Praise for Pe

'A striking debut, assured in voice anu ~~~r~) ~~~~~r~~~~~~ ~~~~~ stories feel lived-in and real, like haunted houses – charged and strange and sexy.' – **Ellen van Neerven**

'Close your eyes after each of SJ Norman's miraculous stories and what is most vivid and disorienting about them only grows, spreads through you. You realise: oh, it's not over. It is as if you have swallowed a large bell that is now ringing out from inside you. You are caught, haunted, rearranged.' – **Maria Tumarkin**

'This collection of spectral stories is genuinely unnerving, genuinely exhilarating. The writing is bold, slyly perverse, and always dextrous. Reading *Permafrost* is akin to being wide awake in a dream, the stories start possessing you as a reader. Eerie and astonishing in equal measure.' – **Christos Tsiolkas**

'A beguiling collection of haunted and haunting stories, adventures in the everyday uncanny, that grab you by the throat and demand a hearing. Norman is a maestro of mood and their sentences are exquisite. Their ghosts will whisper in your ear long after the final page.' – **Yves Rees**

'*Permafrost* is a rare, dark phenomenon of a book, an exquisite collection of stories that are as gloriously unsettling as they are enthralling. It takes a writer of exceptional ability to create something that will haunt a reader long after the cover is closed: SJ Norman is such a literary genius. Reading their work is like attending a seance where, afterwards, the ghosts never quite leave. I am in awe.' – **Hannah Kent**

SJ Norman is an artist, writer and curator. Their career has so far spanned seventeen years and has embraced a diversity of disciplines, including solo and ensemble performance, installation, sculpture, text, video and sound. Their work has been commissioned by the Biennale of Sydney, Performance Space New York, Venice International Performance Art Week, and the National Gallery of Australia, to name a few. They are the recipient of numerous awards for contemporary art, including a Sidney Myer Creative Fellowship and an Australia Council Fellowship. Their writing has won or placed in numerous prizes, including the *Kill Your Darlings* Unpublished Manuscript Award, the Peter Blazey Award, the Judith Wright Prize and the *ABR* Elizabeth Jolley Short Story Prize. In 2019, they established Knowledge of Wounds, a global gathering of queer First Nations artists, which they co-curate with Joseph M Pierce. They are currently based between Sydney and New York.

PERMA FROST

SJ NORMAN

First published 2021 by University of Queensland Press
PO Box 6042, St Lucia, Queensland 4067 Australia

The University of Queensland Press (UQP) acknowledges the Traditional Owners and
their custodianship of the lands on which UQP operates. We pay our respects to their
Ancestors and their descendants, who continue cultural and spiritual connections to
Country. We recognise their valuable contributions to Australian and global society.

uqp.com.au
reception@uqp.com.au

'Permafrost' was first published in *Nine Tenths Below*, the 2005 UTS Writers' Anthology.
'Stepmother' was first published in *Kill Your Darlings*, 28 August 2017.

Cover design by Jenna Lee
Cover photograph by SJ Norman
Typeset in 12/18 pt Bembo Std by Post Pre-press Group, Brisbane
Printed in Australia by McPherson's Printing Group

The University of Queensland Press is assisted by
the Australian Government through the Australia
Council, its arts funding and advisory body.

A catalogue record for this book is available from the National Library of Australia.

ISBN 978 0 7022 6342 2 (pbk)
ISBN 978 0 7022 6537 2 (epdf)
ISBN 978 0 7022 6538 9 (epub)
ISBN 978 0 7022 6539 6 (kindle)

CONTENTS

Stepmother.

THEY PICKED ME UP in their new car. It smelt of leather conditioner and perfume. Hers. French. Thick. She stunk, as my mother liked to put it, *like a fuckin' pole cat.* Everything about this woman, it was made clear to me, was to be despised. Everything, especially her expensive secretions. It was Madame Rochas, I think, and I secretly liked it. It smelt like the David Jones Christmas catalogue. It smelt like the holidays.

They didn't come to the door; my mother didn't go out. Their arrival was signalled by a single, sharp beep. The car, black and shiny as a leech, sat on the cracked concrete driveway, revving its engine like it couldn't wait to get away. It didn't look right in our scrappy, wire-fenced yard. The two Rottweilers were circling, sniffing its tyres. I could see her face through the tinted windows, nervously watching the dogs, and watching me as I approached. The dogs barrelled up to me, almost slamming my knees out from under me with their joyful heft. I gave them each a nuzzle before sliding into the cream leather embrace of the back seat.

Immediately, she pulled a packet of Wet Ones out of the glove box and handed them to me.

I looked back and saw my mother's backlit figure through the half-open side door. Hair, a halo of black static. Sucking her teeth.

My father fiddled with the stereo. Iggy Pop's 'Lust for Life' came on. This was Dad's driving jam. Track six on the *Trainspotting* soundtrack. It was actually my CD. My older brother had given it to me, at my request, for my birthday. It was perhaps a precocious choice for an eleven-year-old, but I'd seen the movie with my cousins and liked the sounds. She had seized it, seconds after I slid off the wrapping, and examined the cover before handing it to my father with a look. It was theirs now. A special soundtrack for weekend getaways in their German sports car. They showed me the moonroof. It was different to a sunroof, which was what my mother's car had. A plane of grey glass separated you from the sky.

It was chilly. They were in their smart casuals. My father in a taupe windbreaker with lots of zippers and empty pockets. She was encased in a crop coat of black rabbit fur, and more gold than usual. Dragging the tips of her red enamel fingers over the contours of a map.

I never knew how to act with them so most of the time I kept quiet. I felt like a spy behind enemy lines. My silence made them (and her, especially her) even more nervous. I was surly and antisocial. Or *withdrawn* might have been the word she used. When they spoke to me it was loud, over-the-shoulder and over-articulated. The same way I'd heard them talk to Ngoc, their Vietnamese cleaner. When they spoke to each other in my presence it was all whispers. They slipped between the two modes like ventriloquists.

The sun visor on her side was down and in the little mirror I could see her tits. *She wears them like they're on sale*, my mother had said. *Thrust to the front of the shelf. Overripe.* They were permanently festooned with gold pendants. A Buddha from Cambodia. An ornate crucifix from her dead mother. She'd wear up to seven at a time, all clattering and glittering in her cleavage. The size and texture of her breasts fascinated me. They'd spent a lot of summers exposed on foreign beaches, basted in Reef oil. The loosening brown crust of her décolletage contained the globes of soft tissue, like the skin of a baked dessert contains the custard. I thought that maybe breasts would be a nice thing to have. A flesh mantle to protect the heart.

'So, the big One-Two!' my father said, referring to my recent birthday. 'Almost a teenager.'

I nodded. Almost.

By this stage the CD had been changed. It was George Michael singing 'Freedom'. Another one of my father's favourite highway tunes.

To our left, there was the cold expanse of Lake George. Of all the scenery on the road to Canberra, that's the stretch that I always remember. How suddenly the void of that lake appears. It's unquiet country. To the right, a steep bluff, crowded with dark trunks of ironbark gums and grey boulders, fringed with shivering grass. A burnt-out car body. A high fence of barbed wire. Everything silver and black.

There was a storm coming. When we stepped out of the car you could feel the electricity in the air. We had spent an hour following the maddening concentric loops of the nation's capital before we found the turn-off to our hotel. Behind a dense hedge, it was as hushed and guarded as the embassies that surrounded it. Clocks behind the front desk indicated the time in ten different countries. The receptionist's badge glinted. It smelt the way that hotels smell.

You could hear muffled claps of thunder outside. By the time we got to our suite, heavy rain was pelting the windows. I sat on the quilted bedspread of one of the two single beds in my room. The one closest to the door, the one I'd chosen. My twin room was adjacent to their double, separated by a door that locked on their side. They had the minibar and the television. I was happy to be alone but I wanted a Snickers.

'Can I have this?' I made my way into their room and opened the minibar to find the chilled chocolate bars, lined up in size order in their creaseless wrappers. I pulled one out. 'Dad? Can I?'

She was at the window cracking the neck of a baby bottle of Gordon's, preparing a couple of G and Ts. They always had one at this time. A cigarette between her fingers, she looked at the chocolate bar in my hand, then at my father. Rolled her eyes.

My father's face contorted with pity and disgust. 'You don't need it, sweetie.'

The National Gallery, monumental ode to brutalist concrete, surrounded by acres of car park. A banner unfurled down its side announced the arrival of *The Queen's Pictures*, the big mid-year exhibition. A selection of paintings from the Windsor family vault would be gracing the colonies with their presence for three months.

The two of them walked ahead of me, her heels making a hasty racket past the Yolngu log coffins and through several rooms of Papunya canvases, seething with the colours of the desert. Eventually we reached the antechamber of the main exhibition space and found our place at the end of the queue, a heaving congregation of quiet bodies, rain-spattered jackets and damp beanies, inching down the corridor towards the exhibition entrance. There were two invigilators at the door to the gallery, one manning the grunting ticket machine, the other standing at one end of a velvet rope, unhooking it periodically to let punters through in clusters. We waited our turn. My father's arm around her waist. All of us shivering, the wet soles of our shoes streaking the floor.

The faces of angels. Virgin and child. Monarch in profile. From the workshop of. Attributed to. Virgin and child. A woman, carrying a man's head on a platter. Looking pleased with herself. Three strange, Flemish children, dark eyes, skin like dough. Cherries and small oranges. Man with fur collar and medallions. Cleft chin, flat plane of burgundy behind. A king. A merchant. Two women and a man adoring the holy newborn. Virgin and child. The women's hands clasped in prayer. Virgin and child. The man's fingers, pincered, slightly camp, delivering a blessing. The baby cocks one leg up. Virgin and child. Sometimes soft, rendered fleshy, drapery spilling from the body of Mary. Blue sky behind. Others, flat. Sideways, elongated, Byzantine. Peeling gilt, angels stuffed in the corners. The faces of angels. Virgin and child. Psyche exposed on a rock. Two nymphs and a satyr. The worshippers of Dionysus. Women with blood in their teeth. Animal skins. Panels for the decoration of a palace interior. Albrecht Dürer. The muscular faces

of the Black Forest. Death, always, stuffed in a corner. The faces
of angels. The Italians with their saints and the British with their
nobility. Mermaid feeding her young. There are seven of them, all
boys. She has a breast for each of them. Seven breasts. All suckling.
The frothing ocean. Looking pleased with herself. Virgin and child.
This one: Christ child, a beefy suburban toddler. The kind of kid
who would hassle the neighbour's cat. Mary's firm bicep, visible
under her sleeve.

We moved from room to room, like insects devouring a carcass.
I was fascinated by the portraits of European noblewomen. It was
their enhanced silhouettes that held particular appeal. The rooms
were chronologically ordered and every one revealed a new stage
in the evolution of corsetry, beginning with the rigid triangles of
the Elizabethans through to the cinched hourglass of the Victorians.
I was prepubescently potato-shaped and I regretted not living in an
era of stiff bodices and long skirts. I was reminded, on a daily basis,
both of my so-called girl-ness and my failure at executing girl-ness
to the satisfaction of other so-called girls. 'Womanhood' was an
as yet remote and compelling proposition: among other things it
seemed as though woman-ness was something you could put on
and take off. It had forms that were standardised and replicable.
Looking at rooms full of corsetted waists, I felt some kind of relief.
I wondered what it would be like to have an exoskeleton like that.
To always be so upright, to be so held, to relinquish your form to
that whalebone embrace.

She was walking ahead of me. Having shed her rabbit fur, her
flesh was uncontained. The black bodysuit was truncated by a
leather skirt, taut over the mound of her arse. She would pause

every time we passed a religious icon, sometimes going so far as to raise her hands to her mouth in something close to a gesture of prayer. My father was fond of the more vanilla Gainsboroughs and any picture with a seafaring theme. He looked at the tall ships with the same captivated longing as I looked at the Victorian silhouettes. A mutual tendency to indulge in period-themed escape fantasies is one of a few things my father and I have always had in common.

We spent almost as long in the gift shop as we did in the exhibition. They bought a framed print of a Turner for the study. I selected a couple of postcards. Andrea del Sarto's *Red Virgin*. Vincenzo Catena's *Salome* (for my mother). A Gainsborough of a woman on a swing, suspended in a green cave of summer foliage. And from the workshop of Giulio Romano, the glorious seven-titted mermaid feeding her young.

'You can't let her go swimming unsupervised, Marcus. She's a child!'

I was already in my costume, my goggles on my head, ready to tear off down the corridor in search of the hotel swimming pool. They were dressing for dinner. She was sweeping a curling iron through her fine, copper hair. I could smell it burning.

'She could swim before she could walk, darling. She'll be fine.'

She pursed her lips and turned back to the mirror. 'It's not safe. She should stay in the room.'

I saw my chance, grabbed my spare key and made a break for it. My heart was pounding. Halfway down the corridor I turned, sure she was behind me, reaching out to grab me, drag me back and lock me in.

The pool was a slender, utilitarian rectangle intended for executive lap-swimmers. I got in their way.

'This isn't a kiddy pool,' a red-faced man growled at me when I was turning somersaults in his lane. *Kiddy.* There was some malevolence in that word and the way he said it. I retreated to the edge and hung there for a while. He kept glaring at me and shaking his head.

I was always looking for new ways to be transformed by water. I wanted, so desperately, to be a water-dwelling creature, for this to be my natural habitat. I wanted to be able to breathe under the surface, to see down there as clearly as I could on land. I wanted to live a weightless life, always floating. This is the magic of swimming: it relieved me of the weight of my own flesh. In water I was something else.

I figured out that if you exhale all of the air from your lungs and hold it out, you just sink. Right to the bottom, like a stone. I did this, over and over. I wanted to see how long I could stay down there. Resting on my back, looking up at the lap swimmers as they pounded along the surface. Or creeping along the edges like a salamander.

I must have stayed in the water for three hours. The sun went down outside. The trees that crowded outside the long window gradually lost their texture. Faded to black. Until all I could see was a pane of glass with nothing but night behind it, and my own reflection, floating in the empty pool.

When I got back to the room there was a note scrawled in my father's handwriting. They expected to be back late. I should order dinner from room service. It was almost ten o'clock.

I ordered chicken schnitzel and chips and started watching a late movie. It was about a small town in Vermont or Maine or one of those picturesque and leafy American states where horror movies always seem to happen. This small town had been plagued by a series of mysterious deaths. Massacred bodies had been found in the surrounding woods. It turned out that it was the trees that were responsible. The woods were cursed, the trees came alive at night and killed anyone who happened to be wandering through them. The policeman's daughter has strayed from the school dance. Some strange compulsion draws her into the woods. She goes deeper and deeper; suddenly a storm strikes out of nowhere. Her diaphanous party frock is drenched, clinging to her like a membrane. She snaps out of her trance and realises she's in a place where she doesn't belong. She panics. Runs. Can't find the path. The trees stir. Stretch out their papier-mâché limbs. Grab at her. One tears off her dress. She's screaming, running, wriggling out of their grasp. Then one long arm scoops down and lifts her off the ground. She's screaming, kicking her legs, there's mud all over her. There's a close-up: the tree that's holding her extends one pointed finger. Slowly, with relish and precision, it drives this finger through the girl's torso, exits through her flat teenage navel, the music reaches a crescendo, blood spurts everywhere. She screams one more time, her body shakes, and she finally falls limp and silent.

At this point room service knocked on the door and I went to claim my schnitzel. I sat cross-legged in a hotel dressing-gown, my hair still wet and smelling of chlorine, and ate, relishing every mouthful of insipid, ketchup-drenched meat. I watched the movie to the end. There were a few more deaths. There was no way of breaking the curse, which had been laid by a witch who had been hanged there in Ye Olden Days. So they burnt the forest down. But the last frame showed a tiny sapling, breaking the blackened crust of the earth, its tender branches twitching.

After that came infomercials and relentless ads for phone sex. It was after midnight. I rummaged for things to amuse myself with. I got my postcards from the gallery out and looked at them. I opened the minibar a couple of times just to rest my tormented gaze on the Snickers I was not allowed to eat.

I'd noticed her toiletries bag earlier on. She'd left it gaping on the dresser. I had glimpsed into it briefly, but didn't have the courage to stick my hand in. It had sat there all night in my peripheral vision, daring me to upend its contents. In the end I couldn't resist. I fully opened its zippered maw and looked inside.

There was a bottle of Madame Rochas. I sniffed at the tip of the atomiser. That smell was her presence distilled. Suddenly she felt nearby. My stomach contracted.

There was powder, lipstick and frosted eyeshadows that glimmered like fish scales. The chalky, sweet smell of cosmetics. Different creams, all for specialised areas. Hand cream, foot cream, face cream, body lotion, eye cream, day cream, night cream. Ear buds and razor blades. A packet of menstrual pads.

Periods had been thoroughly explained to me but I was still mystified by the finer mechanics. Exactly how much blood were we talking about? Did it pour out like piss or was it more of a drip? How many of these things were you meant to go through in a day? I pulled one out and unfolded it. It was like a big, puffy cotton tongue. I wanted to know what it felt like to wear. Would she notice if one went missing? No, I decided. I retreated into my own room for a private experiment, making sure to leave everything exactly as I had found it.

I peeled the backing off the adhesive strip and slipped it into the gusset of my knickers. I looked in the mirror. Under the mauve cotton, there was suddenly an unnaturally large mound. I squeezed the soft bulk between my thighs. The sensation of an unfamiliar object in contact with my crotch was unexpected and compelling.

I had been a precocious and regular masturbator for several years at this point. As my basic manual skill set solidified, I entered a more experimental phase – always looking for objects or textures to incorporate. I'd discovered that a bunched-up handful of cling film, used in the bath, produced one kind of sensation, and the neck of a hot water bottle, the warm bladder pressed against belly, produced another. Spa jets and massaging shower heads were especially excellent. But this pad – the way it looked and felt, packing out my undies with a visible bulge – that was an entirely new kind of feeling. I lingered to admire myself in the mirror for a moment. Then crawled under covers, lay on my stomach, squeezed and contracted my legs rhythmically around stiff cotton packing until I felt that release, that rush of warmth. Every tiny muscle in the core of my body relaxed. I fell asleep.

Through the darkness, I could hear their voices. On the other side of the thick wall. There was heat in their voices. Were they fighting or fucking? It was difficult to tell.

My eyes flickered open, just long enough to see the time on the clock radio. It was after four in the morning.

The noises continued for a while. It could have been an hour or it could have been five minutes. They reached a peak and then, abruptly, fell away into silence.

I didn't hear the door open. But I remember, all of a sudden, being aware of another person in the room.

They sat down on the empty single bed next to mine. I heard the springs creak, heard the rasp of their hands on the starchy fabric of the quilt. Smells. Not the smells of my world, but of another: the hot breath of whisky and nicotine. Sweat, damp and Madame Rochas.

I could feel her presence in the room like a sudden drop in pressure. She was watching me. Willing me to open my eyes and look back at her. Perhaps she wanted someone to bear witness to the state she was in. I opened my eyes just a fraction. Through the slits I could see her dark outline. The smudged hollows of her eyes. Her lips still caught in half a snarl, her teeth underneath, her breath sifting through them. Her hair was wet; it hung off her scalp, clung to her neck and shoulders. That was the other smell. Rain. I could smell water and mud on her, like she'd been dredged up from somewhere deep.

I fastened my eyes shut and lay perfectly still, hunched in a fetal apostrophe. She kept her eyes on me. I could feel them. I even thought, at one stage, that I felt her hand reach out for me. Not touching, just hovering above the crook of my torso. As though touch were not necessary for her to draw me into the field of her body. Something moved up the length of my spine. The low-frequency hum of her presence, her slow breathing in the dark, slowly engulfed me.

I lay there, frozen in sub-wakeful awareness, for a timeless stretch. I finally heard the rasp of sheets and the creak of her body shifting on the mattress. I opened my eyes a crack and saw her dark outline in the bed next to mine.

When I woke there was sharp winter sunlight pouring through the blinds. I looked to the bed beside me to find it empty. Perfectly made-up, as if it had never been touched.

My father was pounding on the door. 'Check-out time!' he was hollering from the adjoining room. 'Get up, lazybones.'

I shuffled past him on the way to the bathroom. He had folded everything back into his navy overnight bag. He put on his cap and his windbreaker. He looked tired.

The benches in the bathroom were totally clear. Nothing of hers or his remained. There was just my toothbrush, waiting where I'd left it. When I went to the toilet I realised I was still wearing the menstrual pad. It emerged from between my legs unmarked, the only evidence of wear being the crease that had formed down the middle, where its shape had moulded to mine. I ripped it out and threw it away.

The dresser had been cleared too. Her toiletries bag was gone. There was just my father, his overnight bag at his feet, his hands in his lap, sitting by the window.

I asked him, 'Where is she?'

He said nothing. He didn't look at me.

Permafrost.

T HE Shinkansen is spacious and brightly lit. The carriage is mostly empty: except for me, a few salarymen nodding in their sleep, and a family of Americans up the back. Every now and then, muffled by my headphones, I hear the same announcement come over the PA: *This is the Hikari Super-Express.* Followed by a list of the destinations: Sendai, Hachinohe, Aomori, Hakodate. Every fifteen minutes or so. *This is the Hikari Super-Express.* A clear reminder of exactly where you are and where you're going.

The trip from Tokyo takes about six hours. Six hours' worth of tea and scenery, slipping soundlessly past in one long, ash-coloured streak. The houses, the apartments blocks, the mountains, the sky, the sea. Everything seems coated in a kind of residue. Everything seems ready to disintegrate.

I have a printout of Kathryn's email folded into my diary. I know the contents, but I reread it anyway. *What a beautiful thing it will be to see you!* It's strange to have her voice in my head.

~

I met Kathryn when I was seventeen. I was looking for escape routes and she fitted the brief exactly.

I didn't have friends. I didn't want them. High school was lonely, then it ended. As far as I was concerned I was waiting for departure. I was unemployed and still living at home, which at that point was a two-bedroom fibro house on a parched square of land on the outskirts of town. Across the road there was Carvers, a truck stop run by a local family. Behind us, obscured by pine trees and a snare of blackberries, there was the train line. I'd stay up late, watching music videos and smoking on the back step, the silence punctuated at precise intervals by the sudden boom of a passing overnight freighter. Then I'd sleep, late into the day, and spend the afternoons trawling the main street of town. I spent most of my hours in the park or at the library. Sometimes I'd cruise into Carvers for a box of Nerds and go eat them in the gutter.

The town I lived in was just posh enough to have a second-hand clothing store. Not an op-shop (there were a plenty of those). Certainly not a 'vintage' store. A second-hand store. A few steps up on an oppie but not quite self-aware enough to call itself vintage; it was just the place you bought your clothes if you didn't want to buy them at Country Target.

It was called Venus in Furs. It was in a little elbow of a street at the south end of town between a drycleaners and a conveyancers. It was stocked with the usual combination of 1970s nylon, beaded jumpers, old leather and denim, with the occasional older piece turning up — a green 1940s crepe frock with faded iron burns on the hem, a black watered-silk purse with jet beading, maybe a cool band T-shirt. That sort of thing. It was owned and run by a woman in her seventies called Corinne, who was into purple crushed velvet in a big way, voice all menthol-gravel. Corinne was cool. She was slow-moving, often stoned, and hardly ever there.

Kathryn was the singular staff member in Corinne's employ. I would go into Venus's often, faff around looking at shit and never buying anything, and Kathryn humoured me. She was ten years older than me, with a round face, a solid-black fringe and equally solid-black-rimmed glasses. She wore checked short-sleeved shirts with the buttons done right up to the neck and tall boots in all weathers. When she spoke the sound was soft and measured but came from her chest. She was a mystery, and I was quietly but ardently obsessed with her.

I'd usually time my nonchalant entrance to the shop to align with her lunch break, which she would always take sitting down at the counter. It took me a while to work up the nerve to sputter out more than a few lines of chit-chat. To my great surprise, we struck up a rapport pretty quickly. I was awestruck that someone older and evidently *from the city* was so eager to talk to me. In hindsight I realise that she was just as bored and lonely as I was.

My visits increased in length and frequency. I'd collect as many fragments of personal information from her as I could and run home with them, pressing each freshly cut specimen between the pages of what – in my mind – was a growing volume: *The Book of Kathryn*. It was banal stuff, but uniquely fascinating to me in the way that the most ordinary details in the daily life of your crush can be. She had been an art history student. She had been writing a doctoral thesis but dropped out. Dropped out and moved, incomprehensibly, to this mildew patch of a town.

I asked her why she chose this place of all places – her answers were always evasive. She grew up in Perth. She was violently allergic to eggs. She had an older cousin who had played in a relatively well-known Australian post-punk band from the early 1980s. She had been a vegetarian for years but had inexplicable cravings for canned tuna. She had such a quiet, concentrated way of speaking, her words filtering out through her slightly crooked front teeth.

We talked about art. Twentieth-century photographic self-portraiture was her great love and her academic specialty: Claude Cahun, Francesca Woodman, Cindy Sherman, Catherine Opie, Tracey Moffatt. I suspect she initially imagined her interests to lie beyond the scope of a seventeen-year-old kid from a bumpkin town. I remember the look of surprise on her face when I asked her what she thought of Joel-Peter Witkin, an artist whose work I had encountered precisely once, in the pages of a glossy monograph in a queer bookstore on a trip to Sydney. My strategic name-dropping worked. That might have been a turning point in our connection.

We talked about art a lot – something that was comfortable for her and illuminating for me. She had words and scripts and ways of unlocking these images that had fascinated me throughout my pre-internet adolescence, images and worlds I had escaped into again and again, which for me had delivered a promise of another place, where bodies like mine could be powerful, filthy, strange and free. She used words like *abject* and *punctum*.

We had short conversations which turned into long conversations which turned into her sharing her lunch with me which turned into trawling the record store after work which turned into beer and cigarettes on the hood of her car at night under the feathery mooncast-shadow of a jacaranda tree.

She lived in a flat. In the town where I grew up, nobody lived in flats. Nobody moved to the country to live in a flat. But Kathryn lived in a one-bedroom flat on the top floor of a 1970s block. There was something quite exotic about this for me at the time. I'd hang out there a lot.

We'd make dinners and watch movies and smoke and fuck. She kept a fat nugget of blond hash in a tin on her bookshelf, a marked step up on punching cones of skank weed from a buckled Sprite bottle in the style to which I had become accustomed. She had a strapping figure, firm and ample curves, a generous belly and thighs, thick upper arms with a winking overlap of flesh at the elbow of which she was highly and unnecessarily self-conscious. She had a deeply undulating back with a swallow tattooed on each shoulder blade.

Was she my girlfriend? I don't think so. I still don't know. Whatever we were doing didn't have a name – we just stuck to each other, bound by the kind of intimacy that occurs between two people who are stranded in a place where neither of them feels at home. Our whole world existed inside her little flat. In her bed, with the blue sheets. On her dark green club sofa. In records and in books that we lent each other.

We both had trouble sleeping so some nights we'd go walking. We'd walk around the empty streets in the freezing cold and sometimes it felt so lonely it was as if the world had ended. As if everyone had gone to sleep and would never wake up. It was just me and her, in the dark.

I didn't think to interrogate the mystery of her presence too deeply. This shitty town: I knew why I was there, but why was she? I asked her once. It was simple, she said. She needed to get away from the city and everyone in it. She wanted to burn every bridge she had ever set foot on. Not because of any dramatic train of events. Quite the opposite, in fact. She had begun to feel like there was something hollowing her out, like there was a fog settling over everything. She just needed to *get away from the city and everyone in it.*

Years later I would come to understand exactly what she meant. I'd come to understand that this was not a simple answer at all. I'd also come to understand what she meant when she told me that sometimes not belonging somewhere is a wonderful thing. Sometimes it's just what you need.

We hung out for about eight months, in total. On my teenage timeline, that was an eternity.

I remember the night she told me she was leaving. Through some connection she'd been offered a job as an assistant to a big-deal curator in the city. It was the job she'd been pining for throughout her years of underemployed arts-graduate purgatory. An actual escape from the retail precariat, a job with sick leave and super. It was an immediate start, so there wasn't much time for either of us to get used to the idea. I helped her pack. She didn't have much stuff. Just a bed and the couch and a lot of records and clothes. There was some photographic equipment too, an old manual Olympus SLR and a few lenses. It was about time she bought herself a new one, she said. So she left the Olympus with me.

We kept in touch for a while. There were long phone calls. I remember sitting on the kitchen floor, the receiver hot against my ear. She'd talk about her job and her mounting credit card debt, covering the mouthpiece every now and then to yell out to one of her flatmates. Long phone calls contracted into shorter phone calls and finally into: *Come find me if you're ever in town, okay?*

It took a long time for it to dawn on me that I had lost her, that our universe had evaporated. Slowly but surely, she began to fade out, until all that was left was a memory of skin, of crooked teeth, of a solid-black fringe.

Kathryn's impression – etched as it was, so starkly, on young flesh – shadowed me for years. In the touch of every lover subsequently, Kathryn was there. When I eventually escaped and made it to the city, I drank and fucked and snorted and swallowed and chewed my way through piles of bodies, bodies of every age, shape, gender, in a variegated range of recreational and transactional engagements, all the bodies that were available to a me as a twenty-year-old in that now-lost capital at the tail end of the 1990s. That city, the gorgeous living filth of it, when the drugs were still cheap and good, and the queers could still be counted on to wear full leathers in February heat. Even under those mounting, mulching layers, skins upon stinking skins, there she was. Faded, softening, but there.

One day, in passing, her name was mentioned by a stranger.

Seven years had gone by at that point. I was at the opening of a group show in which some of my pictures had been featured, swilling half-warm chardonnay and doing my best to conceal my awkwardness and antipathy towards almost everyone in the room.

A gallerist of some prestige was introduced to me. She offered praise for a couple of my pictures, oblique criticism for others. When she asked me what I was doing next, I told her I was going to Japan. I told her I wanted to travel the length of the archipelago, from the ancient forests of Okinawa to snow-tipped Hokkaido.

'I lost one of my favourite assistants to Hokkaido. She went there a few years ago to research a project. Never returned to me.'

Then, she said her name. Just like that. And with it, summoned an old ache back into vibrant bloom. It was quiet at first, drowned by the white noise and hustle of a crowded gallery. But later, alone and drunk on my walk home, I found myself flooded by sensations I couldn't find a name for.

I still had an old email address. Expecting nothing, I sent a message.

It's almost evening by the time I arrive.

The station is tiny, just one platform and a tobacconist's stand, shut for the evening. There's a little waiting room with a row of nicotine-coloured chairs. The ticketing attendant has finished his shift; he's sitting near the door, his thin white gloves in his lap, eating wakame crackers from a paper bag.

He lifts his head when I enter, dragging my pack behind me.

His gaze follows me as I cross the room and sit down. He looks at me for what feels like a long time. Then he exhales deeply out of his nostrils, closes his eyes, and lets his head sink into his chest.

It's been raining. Outside, the asphalt is slick as the skin of a fish.

I flick through the pages of a book and wait. Eventually, a bus grumbles in. Its windows have fogged over. Shadows the rough shape of hands and heads shift behind the glass.

The route number is written in Kanji, so I do my best to divine its destination. After a flustered exchange with the driver in broken Japanese, I discover that this is indeed my bus. The driver indicates he will tell me when I need to get off. The vinyl seat cover is cold against the backs of my thighs. Cold, with a suggestion of moisture, as though a wet umbrella might have been left sitting on it.

The bus winds through the main part of town, past all-night newsagents and squid restaurants and franchise coffee houses with clusters of teenagers in anoraks outside. It drives along the ocean wall, past the wharves and the massive, red-hulled container ships. Some of them Japanese, some Korean, some from Russia. The bus moves deeper into the suburban outskirts and then out further, along a four-lane highway, flanked at first by car dealerships and then by not much at all.

Eventually, we stop. The driver sticks his head out of his little pen and nods at me, before opening the doors. There's a Family Mart with a massive car park. Next door there is an izakaya, a signwriter's shop and a crepe cafe, with a shelf full of plastic crepes in the window, elaborately festooned with too-white plastic cream and too-red plastic strawberries. Opposite, there is a cluster of houses, one of which I assume is Kathryn's.

She told me to look out for a white house, two storeys, with a big momiji tree out the front. I find a place that seems to fit the description. It's a big house. Too big, it strikes me immediately, for one person.

All the lights are out, and there's no car in the driveway. I wonder for a moment if I've got the wrong building, if I should go back to the bus stop where there was more light and reread the directions. Maybe I should try to call her. All I want is a dry, warm place to put my pack down and pass out. I'm here now, I decide. I'm here now so I might as well knock on the door.

I push the gate open and walk into the yard. The garden is dark and filled with the sound of water, dripping from branches, from pipes, onto leaves, metal, the flat black stones under my feet. There's a row of them, pressed into the turf, forming a path that leads me to the front door.

There's an envelope slipped under the knocker, with my name on it.

Hi babe. I have to work late. Not ideal, I know.

I'm trying to make out the rest of the note, with Kathryn's knobbly biro letters swimming around in the dark, when I hear something. A kind of scratching, coming from inside. It's faint and tentative at first, but it rapidly gains intensity and, suddenly, something hits the inside of the front door, hits it hard, shaking the glass panels and sending the knocker clunking. This is succeeded by furious but muffled barking.

I step back, and as I do I trip the sensor on the porch light. The garden illuminates, the leaves of the momiji dark red and glistening, the turf electric green. The dog keeps barking, growling, slamming its heft against the door. The dog. Kathryn didn't mention the dog.

I'll be home about ten. In the meantime, make yourself comfortable. Keys are in the letterbox and there's beer in the fridge. xxK

I wake up to a solid-black fringe and a pair of equally solid-black glasses, staring me directly in the face. There's a hand on the back of my neck and a smell that I recognise.

'What are you doing on my front step? Didn't you get the note?'

I try to find focus. 'Yeah, I got the note ...'

'The keys are in the letterbox.'

'I know.'

'So, what are you doing out here?'

'The dog. What is it, a fucking Doberman?'

'Genji?' she says, as she opens the door.

An ancient, balding creature trundles out and makes his way down the steps into the yard, one paw at a time.

'He's harmless. He's got about four teeth left in his head.'

'Oh. Genji,' I mumble.

'Yeah. Like Benji, but, like ... Japanese.'

'Uh-huh.' I heave myself onto my feet, rub my eyes. 'Is it late?'

Kathryn cups the side of my head with her hand. With a suggestion of a laugh, she says, 'Yeah, it's late. It's late and it's freezing.'

She pulls me into a hug. Her red parka crackles.

~

The heater is taking its time to crank up. I'm crouching next to it on the tatami, trying to suck as much warmth as I can from the feeble blue flame. I can hear Kathryn rattling around in the kitchen. She returns with a couple of cans of Sapporo Classic and an ashtray. She's taken her parka off. She's in a loose shirt with a fine pinstripe, the cuffs undone and falling around her wrists. Her hair is pulled up under a tweed cap, a Yorkshire farmer kind of cap. Just a few swipes of black sticking out around her face.

She looks exactly the same. Exactly. She hasn't aged a day; in fact, her skin seems even tighter than I remember it, and fairer. Winter skin, northern skin. Her walk hasn't changed; it's the same torpid little shuffle. I've never said it to her face, of course, but her walk has always reminded me a bit of a cow's walk. All languid hip movement and shifting belly. *Has anyone ever told you that you walk like a cow?* It's sexy but it's hard to make it sound like a compliment.

She sits down next to me and shuffles up close so our arms are touching. She smiles and lights a cigarette. I do the same.

'I can't believe how different you look,' she says. 'It's insane. Makes me feel old.'

'I was just thinking the opposite about you. It's actually spooky how little you've changed.'

'Jesus, don't say that.' She slugs back a mouthful of Sapporo. 'What a total cunt thing to say to me.'

We both laugh. Her low, chesty laugh, spilling out of her mouth on a tide of smoke, reminds me of how much I loved her. A pressurised memory, pushing against the inside of my chest. I loved her so much that just thinking about it feels like an asthma attack.

We don't talk that much. It's almost one in the morning and

we're both exhausted, so we just sit for the most part, smoking, sleepily sketching out a conversation. She asks all the obligatory questions: how was the train ride? What did I get up to in Tokyo? What have I been doing back home?

I ask about her work. What exactly does a gaijin like her do for money in a squid-fishing town in Hokkaido? The same thing that most gaijin do, she says. She teaches English at a private college.

She talks about winter. Her first winter she couldn't believe it, she says, couldn't believe how people could live through that kind of cold. It made her sick. It made her so sick she wanted to die. She didn't want to kill herself. She just wanted to die, to sink into the ground and cease existing. It's the kind of deep, frostbitten sadness that you might read about in a Russian novel.

'You might read about it, growing up in the dusty antipodes, and think it's beautiful. So when you're all grown up you run away to the north of Japan, hoping to get a taste of it. Then along comes the first winter and you realise what you've gotten yourself into. Someone grabs your head and pushes it through the ice and, as you struggle to draw breath and your heart thumps behind your eyes, you begin to understand. You can't shake it. With every winter another frozen layer builds up under the surface, a dull, heavy accumulation that you carry in your bones.'

She could move to Barbados tomorrow, she says – it wouldn't do any good. Winter is in her, cold and quiet as mercury in the blood.

She takes her glasses off. Her eyes suddenly seem so small. She looks at me, like a little squinting marsupial. 'Is it time for bed?' she asks. 'You look like you're about to pass out.'

The upper storey of the house is completely empty. She leads me up the stairs to my room. A few square metres of tatami, totally bare except for a lamp in the corner, with a hollow, wooden sound to the floor. Kathryn removes the futon from its shelf in the cupboard and I help her unroll it.

Before leaving she pulls me into her again and hugs me hard. I hold her to me for a long time, run my palm over her sturdy back.

'It's so good to see you' she says.

When she steps out, I move to the window and part the curtains. I look out and see Genji, a dull black mass, slowly circling the yard.

Sleep came eventually. It took a while, lying there, floating on the precipice, conditioning myself to the murmurings of an unfamiliar house. But it came. Sleep, stretched so thin with dreams it hardly felt like sleep.

I'm not sure what time it is. Early, I think. I peer down the staircase into the hallway; the door to Kathryn's bedroom is shut. I presume she's still asleep, so I make my way down the stairs quietly.

The house is chilly and utterly silent. My skin shrinks away from the cold.

I tread carefully along the hallway, past the front door. There's a sunken area around the entrance, the genkan, with a large cupboard full of pigeonholes for storing shoes. It's a big cupboard. Family sized for a family-sized house. But it's empty except for two pairs of leather boots. Hers and mine. Dim light hitting the neat, snubbed toes.

I go to the bathroom and run some water over my face before I head to the kitchen. To my surprise, Kathryn is up and dressed. She's standing at the kitchen sink, with a spoon in one hand and an open can in the other. She's wearing the same clothes that she was in last night; the same red parka and the same little farmer's cap. She's staring straight ahead, totally still, distracted by something. She doesn't seem to hear me approach.

I stand a few feet behind her for some time, but she still doesn't turn around. Only when I say good morning does her head flick into profile.

Her expression is ambiguous. For a moment, her face seems to remain suspended, following a lost train of thought, before pulling into a gentle smile. 'Morning,' she says.

She squats down and scoops some dog mush out of the can into a metal bowl, before depositing it beside the open screen door. She gestures to the stove, where there's a pot of miso broth on the boil. On the table there's a plate of dried fish and some tea.

'Help yourself. I've gotta run. I have to teach this morning. You'll be alright here for a couple of hours?'

'Yeah, I suppose so. When will you be back?'

'Midday-ish. We might go for a drive after, yeah?'

'Okay. I'd like that. Aren't you having any breakfast?'

'Eaten already.' She gathers up a pile of papers and flings her bag over her shoulder. 'I'll see you later.' She heads for the door. As she passes behind me she drags her fingers up the back of my neck and lets her hand rest on the top of my head.

I reach around to touch her but my hand grasps nothing but air. I turn to see her shadow slip away behind the paper screen.

A sensation of ineffable pressure lingers on my scalp. Then I hear the front door click shut and a car starts outside.

I sit down at the table and begin to pick at the brown slivers of fish. On the table next to me there is a cluster of jars and packets. Vitamins. Iron tablets. Muscle relaxants (temazepam). Mood stabilisers (liskonum). Tranquilisers (quetiapine). Neuroleptics (zyprexa). Painkillers (naprosyn).

I open up a box and pull out the foil pack. It's empty. Every little blister has been popped and evacuated.

The screens are all closed, concealing the windows. It feels, for a moment, as though the house is suspended in mid-air. Nothing but white light seeping through the paper, no sense of what might be outside.

The floor is littered with all manner of shit. Papers, open books arching their backs, empty glasses and ashtrays choked up with butts and burnt matches. I step through the debris to the window and slide open one of the screens.

The yard, which seemed so huge in the dark last night, is actually quite cramped. The momiji is more petite than I thought it was as well. Its foliage is sparse; there seem to be more leaves on the ground than on the branches. There's a tiled stoop outside the window, another ashtray, filled with rainwater, and a little bowl full of stones, shells and bits of broken crockery. A little collection that Kathryn must have brought home from a beach somewhere.

It's not raining anymore. The sky is white and vast.

~

Only after I've had a shower, and my senses have woken up, do I begin to notice the smell. I sit down on the couch and a cloud of it rises from the upholstery. Then I realise it's not coming from the couch. It's everywhere. It's thick in the air, thicker in some places than others, but everywhere nonetheless, moving in subtle currents throughout the whole house. The smell of hair. Damp, dog hair. It settles in my throat and there's nothing I can do to get it out.

The couch is covered with hair. The floor is covered. It's all over the soles of my feet, my shirt; I can feel it itching at my face. There is a clothes horse in the lounge with a jumper and a pair of jeans hanging on it. The fabric bristles with a layer of the same black hair that seems to be sprouting from every other surface in the house. Fucking dog hair. Everywhere.

I wash my hands, but every time I touch something more black whiskers attach themselves to my fingers.

I sit on the couch for a while and try to watch television. There are only two channels. On one there's a soap opera set in an office. The main plot line seems to revolve around the frustrated lust between a quietly charismatic young salaryman and his headstrong secretary. On the other there is a period drama. Shoguns and samurai. Lots of navy-blue costuming, very heavy eye make-up and glossy topknots. I sit there trying to ignore the itch creeping over my whole body, and the wheeze beginning to build in my chest.

It's a little after twelve when Kathryn's car pulls in. She leaves the engine on and walks quickly through the garden to the front door, her boots squeaking over the tiled threshold. She opens the door and sticks her head in.

I look up from the couch and smile. 'How was class?'

'Not bad. I was thinking we could head straight to lunch. I'm starving. Are you right to go?'

I grab my bag and a jacket and climb into the pale blue Toyota.

We drive and drive and eventually the highway narrows down to one lane. On one side of the road there is a lake. On the other is a thick patch of trees.

Somewhere behind those trees, Kathryn tells me, there's an active volcano. It's not mountainous at all. It's just a hole in the ground. She has no idea where it actually is. Even the locals aren't completely sure. But every now and then the earth rumbles a little and a plume of black smoke floats up from the trees.

After some time, we reach the sea. It's a protected area; the water is grey and serene. Flat as glass.

We drive around the marina, along the thick concrete seawall strewn with nets. Kathryn winds down the window and a breath of brine and diesel fills the car. She points out the squid trawlers: smallish tugboats with open decks, festooned with hundreds of tungsten light bulbs. Huge light bulbs, the size of footballs, rigged up above the decks.

'That's how they catch them,' she tells me. 'Squid are attracted to light. The trawlers head out after dark, turn the lamps on and up they come, straight into the net.'

Next to the marina there's a cluster of clapboard buildings. Most of the doors are shut. They give the impression, in fact, that they have been shut for a long time. But one of them is open. Some kanji are handpainted on the wall above it, and there's a ceramic tanuki figurine outside, holding a fish under one arm, beaming up at everyone who crosses the threshold.

We park outside and go in.

The chef and Kathryn chat in Japanese over the counter as he prepares our lunch. He talks away while his hands move around on the bench, confidently disembodied, carving slices off a glistening slab of raw tuna. He passes the pieces over to us, one at a time, and we eat them with our fingers.

Kathryn turns to me every now and then to translate selected highlights of their conversation. He's just returned from the United States. His mother lives there, with her American husband.

The trip got him thinking a lot about death, he says. How different it is in America. They bury you, and it's all over. Forgotten. It's different in Japan. The dead are with you always. When you speak of a dead person, you should speak as though they are in the room with you. As if they're over your shoulder. If you have a party in your house, for New Year's or anything else, you should leave a cup of sake and some food out for your ancestors. These things are important, he says. For him, at least. Maybe not so much for the younger generation, but what the hell do they know about dying?

He is upset to think of what will become of his mother. She's very old. It's likely that he will never see her again, and she will not be buried in Japan. He wonders if anyone will bother to speak to her after she dies, pray for her, pour her a cup of sake on New Year's.

I take a closer look at his hands and realise that the bridges of his index fingers are swaddled in bandaids. It seems unusual for a sushi chef of his age and experience, a man who has spent his whole life handling knives, to have cuts on his hands.

Kathryn sees me looking, and when the chef turns his back for a moment, she leans in to me. 'He has tumours in both eyes. He's going blind.'

He returns and continues to pass us morsel after morsel over the counter. Tuna, salmon, kingfish, saltwater eel, scallops, roe, squid, urchin. We leave with the sea in our bellies.

The afternoon is slipping quickly into evening.

We drive to the beach and park behind the dunes. The wind is up, slapping hard and cold against our bodies as we move over the black sand.

The tide has gone out, leaving behind it a thick collar of debris. Wood, bleached and smooth as bone. Mussel shells. Small, brown ginseng bottles and pieces of broken china. Kathryn walks ahead of me, picking things out of the sand and putting them in her pockets.

I have my camera with me. I take aim at Kathryn, watch her bob around in the barrel of the lens for a moment, then snap. She hears the clunk of the shutter and turns around. Her face is blank, translucent, like an extinguished light bulb. She moves towards me and reaches out. I pass her the camera. She looks at it, turns it over in her hands.

'Is this my old Olympus? I can't believe you still have it.'

'It works. I like it.'

She hands it back to me. 'I'm going for a walk. Coming?'

'No … No, I think I'll just hang around here for a while. Sit on the dunes. I'm a bit tired.'

She turns and begins to saunter off down the sand. She calls back to me, raising her voice over the wind, 'I'll meet you back at the car.'

Her figure moves gradually down the length of the beach until I lose sight of her.

I return to the car to find it empty and unlocked.

I get in and settle into the passenger seat. I'm so tired. I put my head against the window, close my eyes and, before I know it, I'm partially submerged in sleep, slowly sinking, growing heavier with every exhalation.

A dreamless darkness swells up, and I hang there for a while, suspended somewhere close to the threshold – I don't know how long for.

Gradually I become aware of an unexpected sensation: the feeling of something damp and heavy resting on my thighs. My eyes stay closed, my head stays under the surface, but I feel my hands slowly animate and make contact with the thing in my lap, feel out its boundaries, its texture.

My fingers become threaded in something wet and thin, something like weed. There's a solid object underneath. Solid and roundish, covered with a soft and moveable layer, something like skin.

I move my fingers around gently, absently, for a long time. Then, a soft shock runs through me. It's coming out. It's coming out in my hands. Long strands separate from the roots and fill the webbing between my fingers. I struggle to flick it out but, at the same time, I can't stop pulling at it. I want it all to come out. It comes away so easily. I run my hand over the surface; I can feel hard, smooth patches emerging underneath. I move my hands around, trying, through the fog of half-sleep, to get a sense of what this thing might be.

My fingers move upwards and, suddenly, they happen upon quite a different texture. They rest on the edge of something. A seam. Stitching. An open weave fabric of some sort. A Yorkshire farmer's cap.

My hands stop moving. My breath slows down, until I can barely feel it in my chest. There is a deepening silence. We are in an airless space. A space evacuated of everything except darkness and silence. I push upwards, struggle and, eventually, a sharp breath rips into my lungs.

I open my eyes and find myself alone. The car is empty. Outside, it's almost dark.

I open the door and step out onto the sand. The squid trawlers are making their way out to sea, lining up along the horizon like a necklace. They switch on the lamps, illuminating the water and the sky above.

The beach is deserted. I stand alone for a long time. After a while, I begin to feel the vaguest sense of presence to my left. I turn and scan the beach, the endless strip of charcoal grey. It takes me a moment to see it. A still, dark speck on the sand, about half a mile down. A black dog. It looks up, holds my gaze.

Secondhand.

IT USED TO BE an island. A long time ago, when the city map was only a sketch, full of gaps and improvisations. This place, which at that time was separate, was 'reclaimed', as they call it, from the water.

As a suburb it still retains something of an island's strange insularity. It bustles on Sundays when the growers' market is on but, for the most part, it's a drowsy place. As though it were not really a part of this city, not really an inner-city suburb at all, but a fragment of a country town, which has broken off and floated upstream.

It's a real garden district, populated by established trees and Victorian terraces. Formerly grand houses, with their sweeping verandahs fringed with iron lace, and their dark, wild gardens. Houses built, a century ago, for wealthy families. But they were built on land that still belongs to the sea, and the sea asserts itself, slowly but effectively, in the form of rising damp. The mortar that holds these places together is as brittle as shortbread. Most of them are boarding houses now, or studio flats. Some of them are empty. Many of them are condemned. A few of the tidier ones were Housos for a while – most of this area was, at some point – before the Department of Social Services sold everything and moved everyone out.

I live at 5/247 Greer Street. My walk to work takes me past number 265, a boarding house presided over by Anna, a Greek woman in her seventies, most often seen astride the front steps, listening to the horse races on her transistor radio. Then I turn on to Lawrence Street, where there's a couple of Samoan families. After that is St Alba's Road. An eerie street, built up along the water wall, directly facing the harbour. It's prime real estate, with an uninterrupted view, and the houses there are the grandest and most ambitious. They are also the most exposed, and over time the harbour's corrosive breath of salt and diesel has rendered them virtually uninhabitable.

For a while they were fit to be squatted; in fact, number 17 and number 36 were both squats for many years. I had a few friends who lived at 17 before the cops dramatically raided it with a news crew in tow a few years ago. Number 36 fell apart with people still in it – the upper floor collapsed at a party. No-one died but it was enough to spook most people out of there.

The air around these houses doesn't move. The buildings just sit there, awaiting demolition, like a brace of elderly dowagers, enduring decrepitude in their own discreet company. St Alba's Road turns into Sinclair, and from there I walk up the hill, past the Ancient Briton hotel, and I'm on Miles Road, the main drag. I work at number 51. Every weeknight, from six to twelve.

The actual name of the shop is Redfield's Bookstore, after the boss's last name. Though it's not like anyone knows or calls it that. There's no signage, save for one peeling decal on the front window: *ALL BOOKS AND RECORDS BOUGHT AND SOLD.* There are several rooms, receding from the slim shopfront and ending in a kind of excuse for a courtyard, which backs on to a rear laneway and reeks of sewage and chip fat from the takeaway next door.

The rooms get untidier the further in you go. Most of the shelves are double-stacked, the systems of categorisation and alphabetisation experimental to say the least, and what doesn't fit on the shelves goes on the floor. My counter is at the front, looking out on to the street.

I've been here for four years. Like most people who go into second-hand book trading, I imagined reading would be a perk of the job. This is not true, of course. Trading and processing second-hand books for resale is dirty, physical work. It's eighty-five per cent heavy lifting, and what's left is grime. Your forearms get chewed on by book mites, and your nails, hands and nostrils get caked in a strange, greasy dust.

Every time a new load of books comes in, usually from deceased estates or library sales, they all have to be cleaned and processed, and sanded at the edges if the pages are oxidised. ('Foxing' is the sexy term booksellers have for this.) Effectively they need to be stripped, as thoroughly as possible, of any evidence of their previous owner.

Books are objects of incredible intimacy, as intimate as clothing or jewellery. People handle books with their hands; their spit and sweat gets on the pages; they travel with them and sleep with them. By the time the books come to me, they're drenched in the essence of the last person to have read them and this residue is transferred to me. If I have to get through a big load of processing, from a deceased estate, for example, I end up covered in all manner of tangible and intangible filth.

I leave the shop feeling overwhelmed by the touch of so many invisible hands and the clamour of so many inaudible voices. I get home and run a bath, scrub every recess of my body, turn the radio up loud so it fills my empty flat and drowns them out. I have to do this, or I can't sleep.

The clientele are varied. The steadiest trade comes from the backpackers' hostel and the university nearby, and this is what keeps the business afloat. Students come in and self-consciously purchase stacks of philosophy books, which they can't afford and will probably never read, and the travellers keep the stock of battered *Lonely Planets* turning over. Actors come in looking for obscure plays, and then there are the poetry lovers, who browse endlessly and take surreptitious notes but never buy anything. There are well-heeled retirees, who come in with lengthy book-club reading lists and become annoyed when I inform them that we don't have a catalogue, and if they want a specific title they'll have to look for it themselves. Then there is the cast of regulars, who are the bread and butter of bookshops everywhere. Some of them actually buy stuff. Most of them don't.

On weekday afternoons, I can usually expect a visit from Francis. He's an Arrernte man of indeterminate age. Could be fifty, could be thirty. He's always well turned-out in a white T-shirt and blue jeans, which are a little too big and belted neatly around his hips. He's very dark-skinned, but his eyes are an incredibly light green, fringed by the blackest lashes. He's pretty and proud of those eyes, flirty with them. He always calls me 'brolga bird', on account of the two swooping cranes tattooed on my shoulder.

I told him once, 'Uncle, they're not brolgas, they're cranes, I got them in Japan when I was young', and he just waved his hand sharply. 'Nah. You're a brolga bird.' He asked if I knew the brolga story and I said yes but tell me anyway, and he did.

Francis is a scholar. He reads up on mathematics and physics, history and philosophy. He loves all the big yarns – all the stories, myths and legends from everywhere. He lives for them. He knows everything there is to know about the old Norse gods, and the Olympians, the Orishas, the Lwa, the Catholic saints, the entire kaleidoscopic Hindu pantheon, the gods of the Mayans and Sumerians. He pores over the history and mythology sections, occasionally pulling a book out and bringing it to the counter to show me some piece of info he's found, or some especially salacious tale.

He's a big nerd for fantasy and sci-fi too. He spends a lot of his time in the farthest room, which houses all the genre fiction. I rarely go down there to shelve – we stopped buying those titles a long time ago, because the room is rammed full of stock. So Francis gets left to his own devices down there, and we're both happy with that. He'll set himself up in a corner, ineffectively hiding a can of Bundy and Coke under his stool, and plough through whole series of Robert Jordan and Sara Douglass and Terry Pratchett or whatever.

He has his good nights and his bad nights. Nights when his green eyes sparkle and nights when they seem indifferent and opaque – the world just washing over them. If he's a bit charged or in a mood he'll come in quietly and retreat to the stacks. But, inevitably, he'll front up to the counter bang on time for my smoko. I'll hand him my pouch and he'll roll and we'll have a chat.

This is a part of our rhythm that we've both gotten used to. Regularly, during these little pauses, he'll take time to point out features of the shop. The old window sashes, the narrow stairwell leading up to the office with its ornate balustrade, the Victorian plasterwork on the ceiling.

'Will you look at them roses up there?' he says. 'Lovely. I remember them. All up and down this street was houses, this place too, this was a house. They were beautiful these houses, so big, and Housing didn't rip the guts out of them like they do now. Left all the old stuff. The ceiling roses and that. I lived in a house along here for a bit. Can't remember which one it was. They all look so different now. But it had a beautiful ceiling, like this.'

He knows somehow that the back gate is busted and often lets himself in that way. I'll go out to do some shelving in the far room, and he'll just be there. I might not even notice him straight away. I might be in there for quite a while even, and I'll suddenly hear the whisper of a turning page and realise he's right behind me.

I've said to him once or twice, 'Christ, Francis, don't do that. You scare the shit out of me when you just appear like that.'

And he'll say, 'Sorry, love. Sorry.'

He might exit through the front or out the way he came. I'll go down to the far room again to find it deserted, whatever book he'd been reading put back on the shelf, his chair tucked in like it had never been moved.

~

There's Janet, with the braids. I've never seen any variation in the way she wears her hair. She probably put it into those two long plaits in 1969 and it's stayed that way ever since. Janet has a look about her that is somewhere between middle-class hippy and bronze-age bog mummy. Handworked bits of leather and cheesecloth, a dirty beige woolly-mammoth coat worn in all weathers, and walking stick. She has a queenly dignity about her, in a bog mummy sort of way. Having woken up to find herself in the twenty-first century, contemporary reality is confusing to her. The present is unsympathetic, strange, stressful, and Janet is not interested.

I like Janet. She doesn't make the slightest pretence of being interested in the books.

There are always 'shoppers' who come in, make a strained effort to feign interest in what's on the shelves for no more than five minutes, before it becomes abundantly obvious that, really, they just came in for a chat. Bookshops attract loneliness. Seeing as loneliness is such a socially unacceptable condition, the chronically affected are usually conditioned to masking their affliction with pretence.

But Janet doesn't give a shit, and I admire this. She is terminally lonely and makes no excuses for it. She comes past the shop every day on her way home. Comes right in, sits down at the end of my counter and starts talking, as though she's booked an appointment.

A New Zealander by birth, she still speaks with a slight accent. She's from a wealthy Auckland family. 'They're all dead now, of course,' she tells me. 'All of them. All dead. One cancer, one heart disease, baby sister suicided.'

Janet's mother was an eminent neuroscientist and her father was a psychiatrist, so both she and her sister had the pleasure of being case studies from birth. Before she swallowed a bottle of diazepam at the age of twenty-nine, her sister had XYZ list of diagnoses and Janet had her own.

'Two head-doctors in the family and both the kids end up crazy as batshit. Chicken, egg.' She laughs.

Besides her dead family, she has a couple of other favourite topics. One of them is New York City in the 1980s, where she was dancing and painting and taking lovers, and the other is her son, Joshua. Sometimes the two subjects overlap, as Joshua was born in New York and spent the first eighteen months of his life there, before the pair of them came back here, back to 'the Island', as Janet calls it, meaning Australia but also, more specifically, right here, this suburb, these streets. This was where she found herself when she first left New Zealand, and it felt more like home to her than anywhere else in the world.

She says, 'There was a gap in me when I came here and this place rushed in and filled it. This is where I came back to after everything shattered. This is where I came to assemble myself.'

Joshua was born on 29 October, a few days before el Día de los Muertos. His father, as it turns out, was from Mexico City, and always marked the day in the traditional manner. When Janet came home from the hospital with her son, the fiesta was well underway in the apartment; the father of her child and a number of his fellow diasporic Chilangos were gathered in the kitchen, and the table was laden with marigolds and ofrendas, sugar skulls and loaves of pan de muerto, baked in the shape of babies in swaddling cloth. The apartment smelt of fresh bread, tobacco, aniseed and candlewax. There was so much talk and laughing; there were lanterns everywhere. Her lover kissed her and took the child and held him. 'It was so beautiful,' she tells me. 'So beautiful.'

By the following year the apartment was empty. Her undocumented partner had been deported. Most of his friends were still there, of course.

'They would have embraced us, me and the baby.' But she was too cold, too sad for company. She and Joshua were alone, but she still decorated the table with marigolds, and baked bread in the shape of little babies. Because that was her favourite part, she says. The bread babies.

'But,' she says, 'I'm not much of a cook, you know, definitely not a baker. The only cake I know how to make is English scones.'

She figured that was good enough; she made the bread babies out of scone dough. 'Grotesque.' She laughs. The dough didn't rise in the way it should have, and the knobbly, pocked consistency was all wrong. She ended up with a nursery full of hideously deformed and inedible bread-fetuses. Not long after that Janet decided it was time to leave New York.

So Janet and Joshua came back to the Island. They lived with friends until Janet found a room in a house. The house she still lives in, hanging on, she says, by the skin of her teeth as rents inexorably rise. She's been living on the 'mental pension', as she calls it, for years. It doesn't go far.

Joshua still lives in the area too. He's twenty-six now. Twenty-six and staggeringly handsome. She shapes his features with her hands, as if he was right in front of her. She touches his cheeks and his hair.

'It breaks my heart every time I see him,' she says. 'We stopped speaking. A year ago. I call him up and he doesn't answer. Even when we pass each other in the street, he pretends not to see me. He's my son. He won't even look at me.'

She lowers her voice. 'Breaks my heart. We had a screaming row, and he's never forgiven me. That night, such a screaming row. I did something stupid. It wasn't the first time either, but for Joshua it was the last time. The last straw. A bottle of pills. Stupid. He came for me when I called him. Just like he had done the other times.

I called him and I said, "Joshua, I've had a bottle of sleeping pills and half a bottle of gin," and he came. I was in a haze, by that point. My stomach was turning over, I couldn't see straight. I remember him picking me up off the kitchen floor, I remember his hands and the look on his face, I remember watching the whole thing as though it was a movie. He came for me. But that was the last time. I can't blame him. I'll never blame him. I love him so much – he'd be frightened if he knew how much.'

I saw her once, Janet, in a strange scene. I was walking to work, up Miles Road, and I went past the park. She was there, sitting on a bench. Nearby, on the grass, there was a young man, with dark hair and a sweet face. He was reading a book. He didn't see Janet, and Janet didn't see me, standing on the other side of the street watching the whole thing. I was going to call out to her, but I didn't want to break her reverie. She was absorbed by this boy, who was ignoring her. He kept his eyes on his book, but she was looking at him with utter intensity, her whole body crouched in his direction, willing him to turn around.

~

There's another woman whose name I don't know. She not a talker. But she started coming in not long ago. She's eighty-something, at least; moves with the wonderful slowness of the elderly. She's not frail, though. Just economical: she has no energy left for extraneous movement, so everything is considered.

She's always discreetly but immaculately made-up and perfumed. One of those dusty, comforting old-lady perfumes. She's always on a mission. She's come in perhaps four or five times. Every time it's the same: she asks me, with perfect diction, 'Is there a section for speech and drama?'

I direct her to the plays in the next room.

She scans the shelves very deliberately. She doesn't browse. She's always looking for something.

'I just needed one line,' she said to me once, when she brought a copy of *Hamlet* to the counter. She tapped the book's cover with a frosted fingernail. She said it again, as though it were the most surprising thing in the world. 'Just one line! I couldn't remember it for the life of me.'

To which I replied, '*Rosemary: that's for remembrance.*'

She said the same thing the following week, only that time I believe it was a copy of *The Cherry Orchard*. After that it was *The Misanthrope*. She's always looking for that one line, but she doesn't seem to know which line it is until she's found it. Or even which play, for that matter, so she tends to go through a lot of books before she finds what she's looking for.

She sits tucked on a low stool. Squatting down there with surprising agility. Like she might be one of those old ladies who you see in yoga classes at the community centre, almost definitely an old dancer, can't open a jar anymore but can still do the splits. She sits there with a pair of glasses on her nose, leafing through pages, mouthing the text to herself under her breath.

She always leaves a little pile behind her. Which I re-shelve after she's gone. It took me a while to notice that she was removing the same books every time: *Hamlet*, *The Cherry Orchard*, *The Misanthrope*, and about seven others.

I decided to test her. I deliberately mis-shelved one of them, *The Glass Menagerie*, I think it was. I put it in cookery. That slim little book, wedged between 1970s cake-decorating manuals. She found it. I don't know how she did it, but she did. When I went to check her little pile after she'd left, there it was on top.

That night, as I was shelving them, I took a closer look. I flicked through the pages. Most plays, if they have been working scripts, come to the shop heavily dog-eared and annotated with directors' notes and blocking scores, or, if they're Shakespeare, the bored doodles of high-school students. When I looked closer at this particular selection of books, I noticed that in all of them the handwriting was the same. The lines of single characters had been underlined, as if someone had been learning the part, and the margins were marked with a tiny, feminine cursive. Identical, in every book. And on the flyleaf of every book were the same initials. *JEC*. On every one.

At this point I remembered: a deceased estate, from one of the big houses on St Alba's Road. She was the speech and drama teacher of the local secondary school, a retired actress of some renown in her youth. This happened a few months beforehand. About the same time that this lady, with the perfect diction and the frosted fingernails, started coming in.

I've grown to mildly dread the moment she approaches the counter. Because every time I will have to deal with her embarrassment at the realisation that she doesn't have any money. After all, she's found it, the one line she was looking for; it's there in her hands, at last she can reclaim it. And always that moment when she opens her small burgundy leather coin purse and dips her fingers inside and there is this look of horrible confusion that comes over her face.

'Oh dear,' she says. 'I shall have to go to the bank. I'm terribly sorry.'

I've tried, once or twice, to just give the book to her as a gift. But she won't hear of it.

She smiles and excuses herself with a laugh. She'll come back, she says. I tell her I'll hold the book for her.

'You do that, dear. I'll be back, dear. I'll be back.'

She'll be back.

Whitehart.

I WAS HAPPY TO BE getting out of London. London in summer is no place for organic life, human or otherwise. The winters I can take. Grey, sure. Oily and grim. But nothing obliterates my will to live quite like a packed tube in high summer. It's also my worst season for homesickness. All the hot, merciless stone, the dusty light and the brown fug of the Thames makes me pine, more than ever, for the Pacific. For long shadows and bare feet and endless blue.

Ffion gave me a strange look when I told her where I was going. 'You know I went to college there?' she said, stubbing out her Silk Cut at the feet of the decrepit stone Buddha in her share-house garden in Brockley. 'It's a funny little town.'

'England's full of funny little towns, isn't it? Isn't that what England *is*?'

'Hmm.' Gave me a look. Ffion was a giver-of-looks. Ffion was from Aberystwyth. She harboured a deeply held Welsh antipathy for the English, which I found reassuring to be around.

It turned out she went to college at the Hall where I was staying.

'How did you manage to get a room there? I didn't realise it was open to the public. It's been derelict for as long as I can remember.'

I shrugged. 'They developed it, I guess. Private investor. It's a guesthouse now. Reasonably priced.'

I caught the train south-west, along the water wall that stretches between Exeter and Dartmouth. I arrived before sunset.

The proprietress padded ahead of me down the long, wood-panelled corridor. It was dimly lit by wall-mounted lamps and smelt strongly of beeswax and vinegar.

As she walked ahead, she delivered a practised potted history of the building. Built in the thirteenth century, Whitehart Hall was one of the oldest estates in Britain. During its heyday it was a southern holiday house for B-list aristocracy, particularly those wishing to entertain foreign dignitaries, or mistresses, situated as it is in one of the most picturesque valleys in the region. The noble family that owned the place for centuries began to devour itself in the mid 1800s. The question of the property's ownership languished for decades, unresolved. The Hall fell into disrepair. By the time the twentieth century rolled along, the dynastic dispute had been settled by attrition, i.e., the family, with the exception of an elderly spinster, had all but died out.

The proprietress bit down on the word 'spinster', before adding, 'A keen huntress in her youth', and gesturing to a mounted stag's head on the wall.

I looked at the beast's dark glass eyes. I imagined its last breath steaming from its mouth. I imagined this solitary, aristocratic Diana, her polished boots astride its warm carcass, the cold barrel of a rifle flush to her thigh. I imagined this woman clinging to her life and her inheritance in a single room of the lodge, chucking books from the ancient library into the furnace, dining on venison and hundred-year-old scotch and glaring into *The Well of Loneliness*, unperturbed.

After said spinster's death, the property came up for public auction. The wife of an American textiles mogul bought it, and proceeded to turn it into some sort of colony devoted to the arts and voluptuary living. A place for her and her urbane artist and occultist friends to swan around and get bent on entheogens and have heaps of Thelemite sex parties, I guess.

Ffion had filled me in on what she knew of the history of this place. She'd said the lady of the house had been a member of the Ordo Templi Orientis, and other orders subsequently. That she had hosted Crowley and Austin Osman Spare as her personal guests. Apparently she made a bunch of expensive alterations to the house: secret passages, rooms without doors, which were built under the instruction of channelled entities. Ffion had told me there was a secret well somewhere in the grounds, the very bottom of which could be accessed via a tunnel, where elaborate rituals were undertaken. After World War I, the north wing was commandeered by the state and became an auxiliary hospital for returned soldiers. Following that, it continued to function as a private sanatorium.

I couldn't remember which parts of this story were new and which parts I'd already heard from Ffion. When she was a student at Whitehart Hall in the mid 1990s it was a small but supposedly prestigious art college. A later manifestation of the American Women's Art Colony, with a shaky institutional framework and exorbitant tuition fees laid on top. Ffion referred to it as 'the art farm', and her descriptions of the place evoked a kind of country rehab facility for the naughty, wealthy and largely talentless.

The proprietress continued her chattering on the threshold of my room for ages, fiddling with the keys and looking up at me through thick glasses, which made her eyes seem unnaturally big and watery, before opening the door.

I had been expecting the worst. I find that's the best way to avoid disappointment when it comes to budget holiday accommodation. Seeing as the price of a room at the estate's guest house hadn't been adjusted since the 1970s, I expected the same from the decor. I was pleasantly surprised. It was old, sure. It was kitsch. But in its dowdy, pearlescent way, it was beautiful. There was a lusciously draped four-poster bed. Lots of spindly occasional furniture. A chair by a window that framed, through a grid of leadlight diamonds and wobbly hand-blown glass, a view of the river. The only artefact of contemporary life to be seen was the white plastic wastepaper basket, lined with a Tesco bag.

The nearby township, in the customary feudal order of things, bore the estate's namesake. On my first night, I cycled in for supplies, and found myself at Whitehart Family Stores. I felt strangely woozy.

I wandered through the narrow aisles. Picked up a jar of local honey. Put it back. Picked up a box of couscous, put it back. I spent almost half an hour in the cereal aisle, trying to choose the right muesli.

There were three registers behind one long counter, with three tellers, all of them women in their sixties, all of them fantastically plump and comfortable in their soft cotton T-shirts of lemon and mauve. As I sidled up to the counter they were talking among themselves in their West Country accents: thick, dark and sticky, but with a strange buoyancy. The sound of bubbles rising in a tub of molasses.

As I was leaving, I passed a man in a leather jacket and a cap. He was bent over inspecting a tray of knobbly apples.

'Christ almighty,' I thought I heard him say to the fruit he was turning over in his hand, as though it were a close confidant. 'I'm not suicidal. I'm just trying to have a bit of fun.'

He lifted his head and I caught sight of his face. I supposed he was in his mid thirties. His lip was curled to reveal teeth that were white and straight enough, but with wide gaps between them. There were shadows on his face that looked, at first glance, like dark veins. His eyes were bright green and fugitive, twitching for a moment before his gaze met mine. We looked at each other and I saw the marks more clearly. They were in fact tattoos, hand-done and a little age-blurred. Fine, black filigrees blooming between his eyebrows and extending around to embrace both temples.

There were a lot of heavily tattooed people in the town. That's something I'd noticed immediately. Not heavily tattooed in the Shoreditch sense of the word, though. A lot of people, especially salty older types, had faded bluish markings creeping out from collar and cuff. Both women and men were inked in abundance. Beefy anchors and mermaids. Knives and roses. We were inland, but not too far from Plymouth, so I guessed a lot of these older mob would be ex-wharfies or sailors or other shipyard types.

I'd passed through the market on my way to the estate earlier that day. There was a wiry woman in her seventies selling cheese, dragging on a cig as she efficiently cut and wrapped lumps of local cheddar. She had a rumpled rose on the patch of skin between her left earlobe and the collar of her shirt. The old blokes at the junk store, inert and silent in deckchairs keeping watch over the table of broken radios and mismatched crockery they were not trying too hard to flog, were densely inked from jaw to knuckle. Sitting there, all stone, while day-tripping Londoners and Bristolians pitter-pattered past them fondling trinkets and sniffing at chutney.

But I took note of this guy's tattoos, because they were distinctive. I hadn't seen anyone yet with facial tattoos. They were a different style, delicate and botanical, as if he had vines growing out of his temples. Compared to the sea-dog talismans of the old folk the design appeared either much more modern, or much, much older.

He looked me in the eye, raised the apple to his lips and bit a chunk out of it. Tilting his head back, chomping away at the flesh of the fruit, he paused and looked me up and down. 'You're not from here,' he said.

The comment wasn't really directed at me. He was making the observation to himself. Before I could respond, he turned and walked off.

~

I didn't linger in town. It was a long cycle back to the Hall, along the river and through a forest. The sun was going down and I knew there were no lights along the dirt road through the estate. So I wanted to get back before dark.

The streets were so empty. The tourists had cleared and the markets were all packed up. There were a few traces left in the town square. Muddy footprints; scraps of greaseproof paper trodden into the stones; a solitary, bruised turnip, lolling on the ground. The shops were now closed. The deep-set windows of the Elizabethan shopfronts, glowering under their heavy buttresses, were dark and revealed nothing of their interiors.

Once past the boundaries of the medieval heart of the town, the old buildings became sparser, giving way to the aesthetic realities of semi-rural suburbia. Boxy council houses, roundabouts, scummy bus shelters. I rode past the local high school. Like everywhere else, it was deserted. There was a little kid's backpack, blue with the dancing penguin from *Happy Feet* on the front, dumped on the footpath that ran behind the tennis court. It was covered in flies. I cycled down the hill towards the river.

It was a warm night. I was badly out of shape. Months of sedentary city-dwelling and tube-riding had left the muscles of my legs in no fit state for cycling. It wasn't long before I was dripping sweat. But I pedalled along the riverbank track, propelled onwards by the gentle flow of the river to my right. The water and I were travelling in the same direction.

To the left there was woodland until, just before the gates to the estate, a clearing opened up. There was a smell in the air. It was so thick, and filled the air so suddenly, it stopped me in my tracks. It was sweet. But not fresh. The sweetness of decay. The stink of rot or fermentation. There was a hint of something burnt in there too. Like hops.

I remembered the smell of the old Tooth's brewery in Chippendale, near where I had lived in Sydney. The ghostly persistence of that smell, how it hung so heavily in the air of the surrounding suburbs for years after the brewery closed. But this smell wasn't hops. I couldn't place it, and I couldn't tell where it was coming from.

I propped my bike against the fence and jumped over it into the clearing. I walked ahead, with the bracken and the thistles swiping at my bare legs.

At the edge of the clearing I found a cluster of buildings. They were crouching in a thicket, invisible from the road. I moved in for closer inspection.

One of the buildings was an old pub. Gold lettering above the door read *The Gamekeeper's Arms*. It was well-kept: the front step had been swept and there were young, ornamental birch trees planted out the front, an ashtray by the door. Though the lace curtains were drawn, there were traces of human life. I thought the publican might have been on holiday, or there might have been renovations going on.

It was adjacent to another set of buildings. Older, built from rude slabs of stone. There was a sort of silo and, attached to that, a giant water wheel. The wheel was motionless and suspended over a still, dark pool. Its slats were dry. The smell was stronger than ever. There was an orchard attached. Grizzled apple trees. It was an old cider press.

The ground was scattered with fruit. I walked through the trees and looked at the spoils: it all seemed remarkably fresh. The apples were green and intact. No rot had gotten into them. Nothing had eaten them. I picked a few up. Smelt them. They'd be good for breakfast.

I saw there was a track leading back to the river. Carrying my stolen apples, I made my way to where I'd left my bike.

The thorns had torn into my ankles – I looked down at them as I pedalled. I realised I was bleeding quite badly. It felt fantastic. Soil residue on the soles of my feet. The warmth rising from the road. The fading light: the redolent, honey sunlight of early English summer. My broken skin, my blood. Hot, red proof of the life in my body.

Once back at the Hall I unloaded my groceries in the guest kitchen and retreated to my room. I stripped, gathered my things, and made the long trip down the hall to the communal shower. This room, I suspected, had not been updated since the Hall's previous incarnation as a student dorm. It was jarringly institutional, lit by buzzing neons. Nonetheless my shower was exquisite. I turned the water up scorchingly hot, relished the sting of it running over my grazed ankles.

As I dried myself the stinging on my legs continued, a sensation I assumed would abate. A prickling all over my legs – just flushing, I thought, from the heat of the water. But as I lay on my bed, trying to read, I realised it was spreading. And intensifying.

I got up and looked in the mirror and assessed myself for

visible marks – nothing, no redness even, nothing other than the little ankle bands of minor scratches from the thistles. The blood was gone now, though the wounds were still fresh and pink. But the sensation was all over my legs, right up my thighs. It was a penetrating, buzzing kind of sting, as though my skin were conducting an electric current.

The pain quickly ramped up to a searing intensity. The kind of stinging feeling you get from a bull-ant bite, but somehow it was all over me, distributed over the entirety of my lower body. I felt a rush of panic: was there something in the water? Some noxious chemical residue in the ancient pipes of this place? What the fuck was doing this to me? Had I burnt myself? The mirror revealed nothing. My skin looked fine but the pain was incredible and only increasing, thousands of sharp, invisible shards driving into my skin.

I couldn't find the proprietress anywhere. The foyer was empty. I dinged away at the bell on the counter to no avail. I rummaged behind the counter for a first-aid kit. A phonebook to call the hospital. Something, anything. Nothing. All the cupboards were locked.

I headed back down the corridor and knocked on every door as I went. No-one. I was nauseated with pain by that stage. I couldn't decide whether I wanted to scratch, scream, piss myself, throw up or all of the above.

When I got back to my room, my mobile was ringing. I grabbed it.

'Yes?'

'Hiya.' It was Ffion. 'How's it all going then? Restorative?'

'Fucked.'

'What?'

'I'm fucked. I've done something to myself. There's no-one here to help me.'

'What do you mean you've done something to yourself?'

I explained.

'Ah,' said Ffion. 'Nettles.'

'Pardon?'

'Nettles, babe. You been tramping through any fields today?'

I remembered the clearing. Trudging through undergrowth, the long, whip-like strands clutching at my legs. I thought it was bracken. But I'm no weed expert, at least not on this island.

'Are you serious? I literally cannot believe how much this hurts.'

'Hmm. It does sting.' Her tone is matter-of-fact, slightly bemused. She's crunching on something. 'A fun fact for you: do you know that Victorian dominatrices used nettles in scenes? Used to wrap them around people's nutsacks and stuff.'

'That is fascinating but I need help, Ffion.'

'The leaves are also medicinal. You can brew them into a tea – they are an amazing diuretic.'

'Please tell me how I make this fucking stop, Ffion.'

She paused. 'The only remedy I know of is dock leaves. You need to make a poultice out of dock leaves. You need to go and pick some. Find them around oak trees.'

'A poultice? What the fuck arcane shit even is a poultice?

Are you seriously telling me I have to go out into the forest right now to forage for a fucking medicinal weed?'

She confirmed that was the case.

Moments like this hooked into a very particular, complex vexation I had with the British. I loved the fact that so many people, particularly outside of major cities, possessed such a proud knowledge of folk medicine and bio-regional herbcraft, which stretches its tendrils back to pre-Roman times. I admired and respected this lore and the manner in which it was kept, as working knowledge in the lives of ordinary people. But, right then, I also really wanted to know why I couldn't just buy something from the chemist.

'You know that *Guardian* lift-out I have on the fridge? With all the herb illustrations on it? The big flat ones on the top right. I'll send you a pic so you know what you're looking for.'

I climbed over the stone wall that separated the clipped grounds of the Hall from the woods beyond. I couldn't see further than the halo of light cast by the torch. The ground was covered with shrub ivy. I had to place my feet carefully to avoid entangling myself in the network of tough vines beneath the leaves. I looked back in the direction of the Hall; the only light I could see on in the building was my own bedroom's. It seemed very far away. I hadn't strayed more than a hundred metres from the entrance, but nonetheless I felt the dark of the forest closing around me. The beam of my torch skittishly roamed the shrubbery.

I moved further and further down the slope. I could tell I was getting close to the river. I couldn't see it but I could smell it, and sense its shadowy motion. There was a drop in temperature; the coolness and moisture of nearby water was suddenly in the air.

I found what I was looking for. Just shy of the riverbank was a statuesque and perfectly solitary oak tree. The solid, brown trunk was wearing a little frilly valance of leaves that matched Ffion's photo.

I was bent over ripping armfuls of the things out of the ground when I heard something. Something moving in the darkness behind me. Fear, quick and cold as a steel blade, shot through my flesh. I froze. Listened.

Then I spun around, shining my torch into the thicket. I remember, first, the light on the silver skin of the birch trees – how they glowed. Then I remember a pair of eyes, glinting like marbles.

About ten feet away, standing knee-deep in the ivy, was a young stag. His antlers were stout and pale; they sprouted from a silky lick of hair on the top of his head, which extended down to a point between his brows. His hide was the colour of the birch trees that surrounded him. Incandescent silver.

I was shining the torch right at the animal, but he appeared in no way startled. I expected him to charge. But he didn't so much as stamp his hooves. He was looking at me, composed and authoritative. I looked back.

It was a fleeting encounter. There was a moment, just a moment, when we were there together. But that passed quickly, and the stag, feeling clearly that his point had been made, disappeared. I don't remember whether he ran or ambled. I don't remember the manner of his departure at all. Only that one minute he was there, and the next, he wasn't.

I climbed back up the slope and over the wall to find the door to the Hall open, as I had left it.

The stag followed me up to my room. It was not an image but a feeling that lingered.

Late into the night, I was lying awake on an outstretched towel, my legs marinating in a bitter pesto of minced weeds, which was gradually leeching out the sting of the nettles. I couldn't shake this strange, inchoate sensation. A sense of having disturbed something. Of trespass. Who had trespassed against whom was not clear.

It was swelteringly hot up in the eaves of the old hunting lodge, but I slept with the windows closed.

The next morning I woke up feeling heavy, slicked with sweat, twisted and sticking to the bed sheets like a moist ham hock in a sack. It had been a disturbed night.

I went down to the breakfast room to find everything immaculately laid out for me. Cut crystal, polished silver, bone china, pressed linen. The box of muesli I had bought the night before incongruously plonked in the midst of it all.

I sat there blearily eating and sipping my tea, ruing the absence of coffee, and it became obvious, looking around the room full of tables, all of them empty except mine, that I was the only guest. Everything was still.

I remembered the bag of apples I'd put in the guest kitchen. I went and found them on the bench where I'd left them, in a plastic bag with a knot tied at the top. But over the course of the night, something had happened to them. The bag had inflated. Puffed up like a bladder with expelled fruit gases. It wheezed a thick stench in my face when I opened it. Overnight, the fresh apples I had brought home from the cider house had rotted almost to pulp. Sulking in their juices at the bottom of the bag, completely brown, the skins collapsed inwards on the liquefying flesh. I dropped them in the bin and they hit the bottom with a wet thud.

I went back to my muesli and continued eating. My palate was still haunted by the stink of rot. I could taste it in every mouthful.

I went out for a walk.

I followed the ancient stone wall down the hill towards town. It was still early. Overnight, there had been a sudden change in the weather. That morning, it could have been autumn: the air was cool. The valley was crouching under a heavy grey blanket of mist. I couldn't see far beyond the edges of the road.

I wanted to walk and luxuriate in the cool, uninterrupted quiet of early morning. I had left the city in search of it, needing it like oxygen. I wanted calm. I wanted to be still, for my body to settle into the present like a polished rock in a riverbed. It had felt, riding my bike up the hill in the heat the night before, like the peace I craved was within my reach. I felt the same that morning. But there was something preventing me from fully relinquishing. There was something watching. Dirt has sentience – it knows its own. The valley allowed me to move through it and breathe its air, but it regarded me with circumspection. There was some concentrated power in the place that was palpable and not entirely welcoming to outsiders.

I had been walking for a while before I became aware of another body moving through the mist. The undergrowth shivered. I could hear footsteps and the creak of leather coming up the forest slope, to my left. I paused, looked into the silver depths. Someone was moving towards me through the trees. It was a man. I had seen him before – the previous night, at the grocery store, inspecting the apples.

Cast downwards under the rim of his cap, his face appeared much smoother and finer featured than I remembered. Pale skin pulled tight over his hircine bone structure. Temples and brow blooming with ornate black linework. There was magic in those tattoos. They altered his humanity. Made him into a strange and beautiful animal.

He saw me. At first he seemed hostile. Paused, sniffed. When he realised I wasn't a predator he moved closer. He stepped over the wall and onto the road, keeping his eyes hard on me. He had a dog with him, a mastiff, lumbering by his side.

'Hiya,' he said as he passed, pushing the word through his teeth like a pip. After this brief acknowledgement, he cast his gaze downward again and kept walking.

I discreetly followed behind him. Fell into the rhythm of his swagger. He had a sack slung over his shoulder. It looked heavy, and his body pitched to accommodate its weight.

I followed him through the gates of the estate. The river on one side, the woods on the other. The sparse, slender shadows of birch trees. Then, out of nowhere: that smell. The same sweet, burnt smell that had stopped me in my tracks the previous evening. We had reached the clearing.

For a moment, I looked away. I could hear the river, and my eyes shot off in the direction of the sound. I'd only taken my eyes off him for a second, but when I looked back he was gone.

It was disconcerting. I had lost my one fixed coordinate in the sea of grey. Then, behind me, I heard his voice.

'Oi!'

I spun around. I couldn't see him.

He spoke again. 'Where are you going?'

I didn't know how to reply. I cast my response into the fog. 'Nowhere.'

'Come on, then.'

I heard the creak of a hinge. I looked to my right and realised I was standing before an open gate. I went through, followed the footsteps I could hear up ahead. I was back at the cluster of buildings: the pub, the old cider press.

The walls of the Gamekeeper's Arms were as thick as a tomb and the air inside was cold. As soon as I stepped through the doorway I felt the chill go straight to the crook of my spine and linger there. The ceiling beams almost grazed my head they were so low. The lace curtains, hanging from their rails like cauls, diffused what little light was coming in.

I could smell blood. Meat. The dog was in the corner, bent over its bowl. Happily grunting and crunching bits of bone. The meat was steaming and pungent, as though it had been cut straight off a fresh kill.

The man was behind the counter, looking straight at me.

'Brew?' he said.

I furrowed my brow. 'What?'

'Do you want a cup of tea?'

I nodded. Sat down. The sack he had been carrying was sitting, not far from me, on the bar. I glanced at it. Then I looked at his face.

At close range, I was struck again by the paleness of his eyes, which made the markings on his face seem darker, fresher. Then I looked at his hands. Traces of black under the nails, burgundy in the cuticles. He'd had his hands in something messy that morning. The tips of his fingers were splayed out across the counter, arrested at the knuckles by cut-off gloves. There was something not quite right about their arrangement. It was when I saw the slightly awkward way he handled the teabags that I realised the middle finger on his right hand was missing.

'So what are you, American?'

'No.'

'You're not English.'

'I'm Australian.'

'Oooh.' He cooed theatrically. As if I'd just announced myself to be a really exotic species. 'Osstralian.'

Beyond that, there was no attempt at polite conversation. We drank our tea from battered tin mugs. He rolled himself a cigarette and slid the pouch across the counter to me. We weren't trying to impress each other. But it was a contest of sorts. I got that sense immediately. We stared at each other intensely.

Without taking his eyes off me, he called out, 'All done are you, Scout?' as the mastiff, with a loud snuffle and a shake of its jowls, finished its breakfast. 'Good boy.'

He smiled. Continued staring me down. I continued staring back. He laughed. A low, soft laugh, barely audible.

'This is one of the oldest pubs in the country, this one.'

I'd never encountered a pub or a publican in the British Isles who hadn't made that claim. But by the look of the place, I believed him. The flagstones had been polished by centuries of foot traffic. The black earth pushed up between them. In the quiet, you could hear the building talking to itself. Little noises, little songs. Creaks and rattles.

'And the apple trees, and the old press. That orchard's been here longer than the Hall. It's ancient.' He glared at me, stubbed out his cigarette. 'And it's private property. By private, what I mean is, it's mine.'

He took me by surprise. Had he been home the day before, hiding in an upstairs room, watching me rummage in his orchard?

I shrugged and minced. 'Oh. Sorry.'

'No apologies,' he said. 'Just don't let me catch you in there again. I saw you in there yesterday, there was light and I could see you, could see you were just in there scrumping my apples. But go in there at night again and you might end up negotiating with a shotgun. Right?'

I nodded. There was a pause.

He took a long slurp of his tea. Swallowed, curled his lip. Softening, he asked: 'They feed you up at the Hall, d'they?'

'What? No. Self-catering.'

'Come back at suppertime then. Wouldn't know by the murk but it's the summer solstice today. I'm cooking.' He cleared the mugs away. 'I'm no chef, but I can feed you.'

With that he got up. Picked up his mysterious sack and slung it over his shoulder. The dog hauled itself up from the patch of floor it had been occupying at his feet and trotted behind him as he made his way for the door at the back, which I supposed led up to his flat.

Before disappearing, he turned and looked at me one more time. 'Suppertime,' he reiterated, and slipped into the dark hallway.

I carried his scent on me for the rest of the day. I couldn't rid myself of the sense of his presence. Had no desire to rid myself of it. My only desire, in fact, was to get closer. Where this desire came from, I had no idea. All I knew was, under the layers of black hide and rough wool, there was a body, and I wanted it. I wanted to skin him. Suck the marrow out of his bones. The feeling simmered and rose to the boil, rich and fragrant. Suppertime. Suppertime. I was fucking starving.

The Gamekeepers Arms, by night, was a beacon in the thicket. The hearth was alight. There were people. Old-timers. It was that sort of pub. The cheese woman was there, the one from the markets with the rose on her neck. She had a pint of stout in the grip of her bony hand. There were men, sitting like stones in small clusters. Nobody moved or spoke, but I felt every eyeball in the place swivel in my direction as I walked in.

He was in his spot behind the bar. His hat was off, revealing a head of closely cropped hair. Thin and incredibly pale. I wondered if he was a bottle blond or if it was natural. The icy blond of northern Europe. Sub-zero blond. Silver. Silver eyes. High, polished temples, laced with black.

I sat down. He smiled. Pulled me a pint of rough cider.

As promised, I was fed. He handed me a plate of what looked and smelt like dog food.

I had been vegetarian for more than a decade. It wasn't so much for ethical reasons. I just grew up eating a lot of overcooked chops and grew to hate meat. The smell and the texture of it just made me gag. I'd travelled through some of the most carnivorous parts of the world always managing to subtly deflect the hospitable offerings of generous hosts. Once or twice I had taken a mouthful of something by mistake and found myself sick for days. No part of the prospect of eating flesh had been even remotely appetising. Even bacon, the bête noire of vegetarians everywhere, held zero appeal.

For reasons I could in no way fathom, I found myself tearing into this meal like it was life itself. It was dense, bloody, a little smoky. Webbed with hardened fat and sinew. Parts of it were quite elastic and chewy, like rubber tubing. My herbivorous jaw was maladapted to chewing on animals. I felt myself becoming flushed in the face with the combined effects of effort, the preternaturally strong cider, and the unique heaviness of bloody flesh in my mouth, my throat, my gut.

I sat there afterwards quite dumbfounded. I had eaten the whole plate in a kind of fugue. I could call it pleasure, but it wasn't.

It had nothing to do with pleasure. I felt a strange numbness fall over me. I looked down at my empty plate. Scanned myself for a reaction.

I didn't even know what it was. It wasn't like any reference point I had in my mind for what meat should taste like. I know the taste of beef or lamb. It wasn't even close. I know the gamey taste of very fresh kangaroo, and maybe it came close to that. Not the flavour itself but something else. It tasted … wild. It tasted like a beast. You could taste the breath of the forest on its skin and the tension in its muscles and the course of its blood, and you could taste its last moments of life and you could taste the hands that killed it.

'Venison,' said the tattooed man. As if reading my mind. 'The heart.'

I wiped my mouth.

'I'm not one for offal, personally. The dog gets the squiggly bits, except for that. The heart's good for a stew.'

I drank pint after pint of cider. Apple skins swilled in the liquid and clung to the sides of the glass.

Closing time.

We sat out the front for a while with our glasses. He was wolfing down his dinner, the last of the heart stew. He ate it straight from the pot it was cooked in, which sat on the ground between his legs.

It felt so remote, so quiet. I knew the edge of the motorway was not more than a kilometre away. But nothing of its light or noise penetrated the forest.

He gestured to the ring of neatly planted birch trees that skirted the front yard of the pub. 'I put all of them in.'

They were tall, well established. I would have thought them to be way more than thirty years old. As old if not older than him.

He repeated himself, pointing to them with the tip of his fork. 'I planted them. That's a guardian tree – the silver birch.'

I mentioned a book that was given to me when I was a kid. A reprint of an old book on faerie lore. It was a present from a mad, witchy aunt in the Yorkshire Dales, my father's first cousin, on my first-ever trip to England when I was nine. There were chapters in there on the significance of certain trees. Everything was lushly and imaginatively illustrated. The birch tree always scared me, I told him. Whenever I was looking through the book, I'd be careful not to so much as open the page that listed it. The birch spirit, according to that book, was a malevolent spirit.

'The one with the White Hand,' he concurred.

'Yes. The White Hand.' That was the name they had for it. The touch of the White Hand to the forehead meant madness. A touch to the heart meant death. Birchwood, like rowan or hawthorn, should never be burnt. The exact words of that book, a forgotten tome of my childhood, rang in my ears.

We went around the back, into the orchard. The moon was bright; we could see each other clearly. We stepped close to one another until our torsos met. For all his bravado, he was suddenly quiet. I slipped my hands under the heavy lapels of his leather jacket and found the curve of his waist – his body was thick but firm, with a girlish flare at the hip. He was still as I touched him, as though he were allowing himself to be inspected.

I ran my hands over his flanks, over the warmth of his back, his cotton shirt – damp with acrid sweat, the stench of him rising from that warm place between heavy leather and skin. The fabric rippling under my palms as I gathered it; my fingers finding the edge of his belt, finding the skin underneath, following the ridge around to his belly.

My hands grazed over his chest and came to rest on his jaw. I pulled his face closer to mine, but did not kiss him. Held my mouth to his, open, barely touching, our breath commingling, the funk of cider and meat and nicotine. I gripped his scruff with one hand while the heel of my palm pressed lightly, rhythmically against the seam of his crotch.

I stood back. Without instruction, he stripped. He was fantastically hairy. Remarkably, the hair that covered his body was as white as the hair on his head.

I remember leaning against the trunk of an apple tree while I held his head, pushing his face hard into me, his hands gripping my hips while I came the first time in his mouth. I came again on top of him, my knees in the dirt.

I was feeling horny and reckless enough to fuck him raw. I remember the taste of myself on him as I choked down the length of his cock, and I remember the way his hips went loose at the hinges when I found his hole, first with my mouth and then with two spit-slicked fingers. He looked at me when I entered him, and smiled. It was a goading kind of smile. The wry, slutty smile of someone who knows exactly how much they can take.

He said, 'Let's go upstairs.'

His room was what I expected: spartan. Basic, but orderly. A thin mattress on the floor, very little in terms of personal effects. A pair of boots, a small chest of drawers and, leaning in the far corner, the slender silhouette of a hunting rifle. I'm not nervy around guns – my older brother used to shoot pigs; he had five rifles mounted in his room.

Nonetheless he clocked that I clocked it, and quickly said: 'It's not loaded.' I did flinch when he reached for it, a little too swiftly, only to open the chamber to show me. 'See? Empty.' Then handed me a bottle of lube and said: 'I've got gloves if you want, but I'm clean.' Then lay himself down. Lit up by a bright bolt of moonlight.

I did kiss him, then. I kissed him long and deep while I worked two fingers, three fingers, four fingers into him. As I felt him yielding, opening around my hand, I pulled my mouth away from his and sat upright between his splayed legs, pinning his thigh down with my left hand while my right moved deeper and deeper into him. He barely made a sound as I fucked him, just long, slow breaths as he melted over my knuckles, as I pushed into the hilt of my thumb. He kept his head arched back and his eyes closed until that moment – that most delicious of moments, that tender threshold – when he lifted his head and looked at me directly. Nodded his head a little to let me know that yes, he was ready.

His arse was deep and well practised: he took my fist easily. By the time he came I was halfway to the elbow. The feeling of slipping your whole fist inside another person – the precise moment when another body surrenders completely to receive you – is the second most beautiful feeling in the world. The first is holding it in there immediately after they've climaxed. It's one thing to feel a person's heartbeat through their chest. It's another thing to feel it beating in their arse. To feel a part of your own body completely engulfed in another's aliveness.

We lay silently on that thin mattress. In a display of unexpected tenderness, he curled into my chest like a foal.

He fell quickly into a deep sleep. I lay awake for a long time, listening to the nocturnal mutterings of the building. Listening to his breath, feeling it flutter over the skin of my throat.

My nose was buried in his hair. The smell of it was extraordinary. It smelt like the river, like peaty soil and burnt wood. It smelt like piss and semen. It smelt like a crate of apples, stored over the winter, swaddled in straw. It smelt like rawhide. Like an animal's pelt. It smelt like the forest.

I buried my fingers in it and moved them over his scalp. In the swell of drunk, post-orgasmic half-sleep, I thought I felt two lumps on his crown. Strange, twin swellings under the skin. As if some appendage had been cut off, and the scalp had grown over the stumps.

I woke up early the following morning, alone in the bed. I searched the building, but there was no sign of him.

I walked through the creaking rooms of the old inn, ducking under low doorways, calling out for an answer. I descended the narrow staircase into the bar. It was deserted. Curtains drawn. The back door was unlocked.

I stepped outside. The birch trees looked smaller. Something felt wrong. Something churning, unsettled. I realised quickly what the feeling was. I sensed my gut desperately contracting around last night's dinner, trying to figure out what to do with it. A wave of violent nausea gripped me, and I found myself with one hand steadying myself against the side of the building, heaving my guts up. Lumps of meat, blanched and desiccated by the acids of my stomach and too much strong cider, thundered out of me and onto the grass.

The sun was coming up. There was a breeze shifting the leaves of the apple trees. I made my way towards the gate.

That evening, I walked past the clearing, couldn't see any lights on. I waited for signs of life. Sat by the river and smoked one cigarette after another, expecting, any minute, for that man, whose name I still didn't know, to turn up. I even looked in the bushes, thinking he might be in there watching me, totally motionless, waiting for me to notice him. Such was the ineffable sense of him in the very breath of that part of the forest. But he never came.

In the end I went back to my room. I had one night left of my holiday. Perhaps it was best, I decided, to spend it alone. There are plenty of pretty sexy tattooed boys and girls in London. I'd get another when I got home.

I stayed in, packed, read. Went to bed early.

I remember moving down the silent corridor, down the stairs, opening the back door. Then the breath of the night, the sound of crickets. Crossing the lawn in a T-shirt and boots, damp skin, gooseflesh. Following. Following what I couldn't see, only what I could sense up ahead of me, retreating through the undergrowth, pulling me deeper into the woods. Moving through the birch trees. Their long fingers, groping at the night like blind hags.

The river, rolling on, is a strip of silver at the end of the reel. A conductor of light only, empty of images. In front of it, a silhouette of an oak tree. The same oak tree, I realise, that I came to two nights previous, in search of dock leaves.

In the darkness, waiting. For what? Feeling insubstantial. Uprooted from the flesh, as though I have been pulled from myself and brought to this place. Knowing I am awake but feeling perhaps that I'm still sleeping, a few hundred yards away, in a soft bed in a dark room. What part of me have I given up to the forest? What part is awake now and here, dissolving into this different darkness, being drawn into the flow of a different river? Here, breath suspended, waiting.

In the black, I hear the creaking of a rope.

I'm walking towards the oak tree. I get closer and I see it. A cluster of shadows first, a thing without definite shape. Before I know it I'm up close, reaching out my hands. I touch it. It's still warm.

The sternum has been split, the ribcage cracked open and emptied. The huntsman has removed the gizzards and the heart. My hands are on the distended ribs. The hinges of the thorax have been broken; with the slightest pressure I could close the cavity.

Its hands are tied behind its back. It has been stripped naked. Strung up by its feet, gutted and bled. The fine, silvery hide is largely intact. Splattered with blood and dirt and shit, but still in one piece. Its clothes are scattered on the ground. Boots. A thick wool jumper. Fingerless gloves. A leather jacket. The head is missing entirely. Claimed as a trophy. That beautiful head.

I lift my hands to my face, cup them around my nose and mouth. Drink the smell that's on them, as though it were warm liquid in a bowl. The smell of hot life, as it leaves the body. The smell of the transition between creature and meat.

Ffion. Smoking on her balcony. Her upper lip bejewelled with sweat. All around us, London, wheezing in the heat.

'It was all over the news!' she said. 'I couldn't believe it. There are riots in fucking Zimbabwe and the English media are getting their knickers in a twist over a fucking slaughtered deer. I suppose it's a special interest story.'

She was right about Zimbabwe. But it wasn't any old deer. It was an albino stag. An incredibly rare animal. Every other deer in the forest was game, but the White Stag was protected. *Sacred.* A local hunter had been quoted in the paper using exactly that word. It was a sacred creature. They could only estimate its age. It had dwelt in undisturbed solitude in those woods for at least half a century.

On the Sunday morning I had left to come back to London, he'd been found strung up by his hind legs from a tree, disembowelled and beheaded.

'I mean, of course it's horrible. But it's the same thing they do to any trophy kill. The head would be worth a fortune. They'll stuff it and sell it to someone with more money than sense.' Ffion sighed. Dragged on her Silk Cut. Asked me if I'd be staying for dinner. 'Are you still not eating meat?' She was roasting a posh joint. 'It's from Waitrose,' she assured me. 'Certified organic.'

Hinterhaus.

AM. THE EYES OF the city are half closed. The chill hasn't hit in earnest yet, but people are bracing themselves. Those who are left behind, who didn't manage to escape this year and jump a cheap flight to Andalusia or Morocco, are pulling out their black overcoats and hardening their faces against the wind.

In a top-floor apartment in the former East, I'm putting one foot in front of the other. Letting one breath follow the next. Every morning I cut a slice from the same loaf of black bread. I look out at the same view. Hundreds of other buildings, just like mine, make up the glowering skyline. All of them built to more or less the same plan – from above it looks like honeycomb. All those courtyards, opening their gullets up to the sky.

It's like rock climbing, I think I said to you on the phone once. Every minute ritual, every familiar sensation is a foothold in the sheer, vertiginous drop of solitude.

~

I call you, and your phone rings out. Again. And, again, there it is: that horrible pause, the little interval of silence between the last, desperate ring and the diversion to your voicemail. What I want is the sound of your voice but what I get is the sound of your absence, played and replayed.

For you, it's summertime. Early morning. You're there somewhere, in that other city, emerging from a deep, warm night. Maybe you're up already, walking the streets near your house, your bare feet moving over the asphalt. Or maybe you're coming home from a sweaty party. You might be down by the water, or you might be on the balcony. You might be doing your laundry or putting some toast under the griller or putting frangipani blossoms in a blue bowl on the table or opening something or standing on a bit of broken glass or doing some sit-ups.

You might be moving through the world or you might be perfectly still. You might be in bed. There might be a breeze moving over your skin as you lie there, maybe sleeping, maybe chasing thoughts or dreams around the inside of your beautiful skull. You have all the windows open. The wooden blinds are chattering. You can hear the birds. You can hear the phone ringing, and you know it's me, and you're not answering.

This building isn't up to scratch. It's liveable; my apartment is comfortable. But in the context of the surrounding area it's a trash pit. Like most of the suburbs of the former GDR that sprawl outwards from Alexanderplatz, this area has been aggressively redeveloped. It's largely defined by its youthful population and high birthrate. It's where young, affluent urbanites come to breed: there are more strollers here than in any other part of the city, more yoga schools, fewer immigrants and old people, less graffiti. More white. White is the new black. In a city supposedly known, at some point in recent hearsay, for its vast and magnificent urban decay, buildings like this one are increasingly rare.

The whole north side of the building, the Hinterhaus, is vacant. It faces me, dead on, from across the Hof when I take my seat at the breakfast table. The windows have been stripped of their dressings and coated with newspaper on the inside. I don't know how it's managed to escape development for so long. Tucked back here, invisible from the street, I imagine it to be full of unfinished private histories. Or maybe it's just full of black. Gutted by fire perhaps. The bike racks are all empty. The walls are streaked with brown effusions, cornices caked with grit. The doorbell has been ripped out, the wiring hanging from its concrete socket like a severed bundle of nerves.

It's minus twelve outside. I have nowhere in particular to go and it is hardly the weather for a casual stroll, but if I don't get out of the house I'll lose my mind. I put my boots on. They are heavy and a little too big. The last time I wore them in the southern hemisphere was on your property down south. We went for a walk up the stock track after a storm. The ground was soft. The boots still carry traces of that soil, embedded in the little divots cut into the upper rim of the sole. I love putting them on, pulling the laces tight around my ankles.

I step out into the hallway. The stairwell sustains the echo of my footfall as I make my way down; the sound of my own steps follows me. At the bottom there's a small atrium. Telephone wires humming in the dark, the intercom glowing all peachy by the door, bearing the names of occupants. Buscholzt. Klussmann. Keun. Ortmann. Meyer. Erbert. Schott. Weiss. This is a very white German neighbourhood – there's not a single Turkish or Arab name on the list. I wonder who they are, what the insides of their apartments look like.

In the weeks that I've been here, I haven't encountered a single other human in this stairwell. Every name is a mystery, a symbol corresponding to an individual life that I can't access, holed up and sustained in its own cell within the hive of the building. My rectangle is blank. My apartment is a nameless place, inhabited by travellers, rented out by the week.

I walk out into the courtyard. Dirty snow, laced with streamers from New Year's. The smell of burning coal. The sound of bells.

PM. The bakery across the street is open twenty-four hours. I go there some nights when I can't sleep.

A forty-something vintage goth works the night shift. From the hours of midnight to six am, this bakery is their domain. They spend most of their shift draped over the low counter, reading novels and swigging from a hipflask they keep in their pocket. They have bobbed red hair, a home henna job, swept into a glossy side-part, which they are perpetually tucking and untucking from behind their ear.

Even though they work alone through the most desolate hours, with so few customers, they're always immaculately made-up.

Eyes lined with kohl, and a streak of burgundy to bring out each vicious cheekbone. Under the pancake, there's a lunar smattering of pockmarks; their pores are getting wider and the lines on their brow are getting deeper. They might have looked sulky and overdone at twenty, but in middle age, they've grown into a stately paragon of piss-elegance. Their name, I've learnt, is Tobias.

I like Tobias. We have a disgruntled kind of rapport. But they're moody. Sometimes they're cute and saucy and wink at me when they give me my change, throwing in a sweet thing for free. Other times they're all schnauzer; they communicate in grunts and give off an air of generalised annoyance. They're the only person I have regular contact with in this frozen tundra of a town, so their moods affect me more than they realise.

This evening Tobias has got something to be upbeat about. There's a bit of flourish in the movements of their wrists and hips, in the flick of their head, and as I walk into the empty shop they greet me with a chirpy, 'Ha-loooo-chen.' Under their white bakery smock they're wearing their favourite T-shirt, the one with the words *Love Kills Slowly* handpainted in English across the chest.

Coffee. And a biscuit. I point to the tray of lebkuchen in the display case. A specialty of the festive season. Tobias arranges three of the little sugary hearts on a plate for me. I take it and sit at the long communal table up the back.

I eat the cheeks of each heart first. Bite the round bits off a heart and it becomes a diamond. Like anything, first bite is best. Cracking the sugar husk with my teeth, then sinking into the ginger insides. Mealy, like sawdust. Sucking rather than chewing, letting it dissolve into a spicy pulp on my tongue. Spreading it over the ridges of my palate. My lips are horribly dry and cracked. The sugar stings the splits in the skin, and I leave little smudges of blood where my mouth has been. My coffee arrives. I eat my sweets and drink, looking out the shop window at the street.

There's someone out there. A figure standing in the entrance of my building. It's a man. He's standing very still, smoking a pipe. I watch him for a while.

Tobias comes and sits at the table. They top their coffee up with a nip from their hipflask and open a dog-eared novel. One hand picks at the foil lettering on the front cover. I study their fingers. Long. Heavy rings. Two pewter talons gripping an index finger. A garnet on a pinky, an antique. They sense me looking at them. Look up. Raise an eyebrow. I turn away, fix my gaze out the window again.

The man with the pipe has moved on. There's just the empty street, suffused with amber light. Condensation has built up around the edges of the window, an aureole, framing an empty tableau.

I leave my money on the table and walk out. I cross the street, pause in the doorway of my block while I rummage for my keys. The smell of pipe smoke lingers on the threshold.

AM. The apartment has no bathroom of its own. This is not uncommon in prewar buildings – there's a low ceramic sink in the kitchen, which I guess is there for washing pits and bits, but the main bathroom is communal. One bathroom is shared between the occupants of each floor. It's cold and walled with liver-coloured tiles and calcified pipes, but there is something about it. Something perversely luxurious, like an abandoned pleasure dome. This is largely to do with the bathtub. It's ancient and deep and placed, ceremoniously, right in the middle of the room.

I'm slowly pickling in the warm water. The pads of my fingers have shrunk and lost sensation.

I realise, after some time, that I've been singing to myself. What I'm singing I have no idea. I've presumably, over the course of the last hour or so, made my way through my usual repertoire of choruses and misremembered lyrics, to find myself here, immersed in an oddly beautiful improvised melody that seems to have come to me from nowhere. It might be a distorted version of something I've heard before. Some classical thing. Something old and wordless. Certain phrases repeat themselves; from the fragments, a structure of sorts is emerging. I follow each bar to its conclusion and round the corner into the next, savouring the pleasure, which is so familiar and so strange, of my own voice, richly vibrating and filling the room.

I pull out the plug. Let the water drain as I lie there, feeling its downward pull.

Something small and quick enters my vision from the side. A moth. A big one, plump, dusky grey. It pauses on the edge of the bath near my shoulder. For a moment, its wings are perfectly still. Its antennae continue to twitch, alive with minute signals. It looks at me. I hold my breath, keep still, and look back. The plughole chokes on the last of the bathwater.

PM. I try you again, at the usual time. In the usual chair by the usual heater with the usual gutful of anticipation and dread.

I punch the usual numbers into the usual keypad. And, as usual, you're not there. I listen to the throaty trickle of the radiator. My eyes sting.

I go to the kitchen and pour myself a scotch. I still have some valium left, somewhere in the second drawer. I root around in there until I lay my hands on the packet. I push the last pill through the skin of its silver blister and wash it down. I sit on the benchtop in the dark kitchen, drinking and peeling the ragged leaves of foil from the empty pill packet with my teeth. Slipping them up between my incisors, dragging my tongue along the edge, spitting them out onto the floor. Tearing at the packet like a scab, following a sudden, nervous desire to pick the plastic clean.

In one corner of the kitchen, there's a stereo. With a turntable, and a modest collection of LPs stacked next to it. It's generous and trusting of the owner to leave out their vinyl to entertain their guests; nostalgic fancy, I guess. Though, the incoherence of the selection tells me this is most likely not a private collection; it includes everything from Zarah Leander to Willie Nelson to medieval Spanish court music to Bauhaus to obscure Schläger stars and back again. To my surprise and delight, a copy of the Triffids' *Treeless Plain* emerges from the mix. I put it on.

The first three tracks play out. Eventually comes the slinky opening baseline of 'My Baby Thinks She's a Train', plucking and humming through the darkness. My footsteps trace diamonds across into the kitchen floor. Forward. Back. Side. Side. Forward. Flourish. I lift my hands, one of them still holding my drink, to embrace an invisible partner. Feeling my calves lightly tense and relax as I glide around on my toes, I'm dancing a ghost tango.

I pause by the kitchen window and look out. Rooftops. Bare trees. Twin smokestacks in the distance, keeping each other company. No stars, no clouds. Still, quiet, everything cut in silhouette against the greenish backlight of the night sky. It could be a view of the seabed. This could be a sunken city. I could be a solo explorer, kilometres from the surface, running low on oxygen.

I throw open the windows. Lean my body out into the bitter cold. First: cold. Second: smoke. Always, the smell of smoke.

Beneath me, the courtyard, opening like a pit. The gutters festooned with fringes of ice. The bottom is scattered with remains. Bicycles in their slots. A swing set. Outdoor furniture. Black, empty flower beds. A shopping trolley and an old, strict armchair, like a throne, planted in the slush. The north wing of the building, pasted over and hammered shut, stares dumbly back at me.

I can hear something. It's not part of the music. Something else. At first I think it must just be the movement of air through pipes or a crevice, the strange wheezes that buildings make at night. But it's too persistent. And too coherent.

I turn the stereo down and listen harder. It's melodic. Unmistakably a human voice. Singing. The same phrase over and over. Something that I recognise. Some classical thing. Something old and wordless. It's impossible to tell where it's coming from.

AM. I walk the streets like a horse walks on a tether: around and around the block in a frustrated radius. I slip on the ice quite often. I end up on my knees in the pissy, gritty snow, get up, skin stinging hot under wet cloth, and keep going. After an hour or so of wandering in circles, I find myself back in the doorway of my apartment building. I'm tired and cold. But I don't want to go up there. It's four am.

The bakery's open. I'll get some bread for the morning. Maybe have some coffee.

It's dim, warm, smells good. Tobias is behind the counter as usual, leaning against the doorframe between the shopfront and the kitchen, eating a Danish and staring at the floor. I'm standing at the counter for ages. They don't acknowledge me. They continue to pick at their Danish, looking downwards.

'Hallo …'

Nothing.

'Hallo?'

I'm aware that my voice is probably not far above a murmur. I haven't spoken to anyone for days. The challenge of communicating with another human is almost too much for me. I clear my throat.

'Entschuldigung?'

Finally they lift their head and look at me like the sharpness of my tone came as a surprise. Say nothing. Chew, open jawed, on their mouthful of pastry. They're dazed tonight. Drawn and glazed over. I order a coffee and sit.

I pull a magazine from the stack and flick through it. It's a four-year-old copy of *National Geographic*. The main article is something about bats and the science of echolocation. There are lots of pictures of snouty bat faces close up. Multiple diagrams. Pencil drawings of bats in flight, with semicircles representing sonar pulses radiating from their heads. There's a lithograph of a nineteenth-century gentleman in a cravat, an Italian scientist I learn, who in the 1840s began running experiments on fruit bats that involved blinding them with carbolic acid, before setting them loose in an attic with bells hanging from the ceiling. He discovered that the bats were able to navigate skilfully around the obstructions despite being deprived of sight. From this he developed a hypothesis that bats possessed a sixth sense.

I'm reading about the scientist's presentation of his findings, and subsequent humiliation at the hands of the scientific community, when I hear someone come in.

It's a man who must be in his eighties. He walks slowly across the room, towards the table. He's dressed in the style of his youth. Thrift elegance. Tailored trousers, hat, leather-soled boots. He removes his hat to reveal a high, glossy pate. What's left of his hair clings to his head like lint clings to a lozenge found in the pocket of an old coat.

He reaches the table and, without a word or a gesture, sits down directly opposite me. There are about fifty empty seats at the table but he chooses that one. He doesn't acknowledge me, even though he's chosen to sit at an uncomfortably close range. I can feel his knees almost grazing mine under the table. He settles into his seat.

It's only then that I notice, through the parting lapels of his jacket, that his chest is bare. Ribbed and concave, pale to the point of translucence. He wears braces that form a parenthesis either side of his grey nipples. There are dark marks and surgical scars. He's had some kind of major thoracic operation: there's a pale ridge dividing his sternum, and another one, smaller but much deeper, more like a puncture wound, at the base of his throat.

Tobias comes over and sets my tea down on the table. I hand them my change. They ignore the old man and disappear into the kitchen.

I can't take my eyes off that bare chest. The filmy skin and the pronounced ribs remind me of a white lungfish. His breath is desperately laboured; his whole body seems engaged in the struggle to inhale. Wherever he's come from, the exertion of the journey has been too much for him. And the cold. It's minus nine outside. That bare skin. He seems, in fact, to radiate cold. I can feel it coming from him, condensing in the air around him.

He starts pulling smoking paraphernalia out of his pockets. Slowly, one object at a time, placing them on the table: a tin of tobacco, a tamper, a chestnut pipe, a lighter. I watch his hands as he chops and packs. There's another object on the table. A glass tube, full of chaffy, grey stuff. He sprinkles a bit of it into the pipe on top of the tobacco and packs it down. I wonder what manner of kicker he's adding to his smoke, what kind of archaic substance this ancient opium eater has access to.

Tobias ignores him. He doesn't order anything, doesn't speak, doesn't look at me or anyone. He's still there when I leave, dragging on his pipe.

I get home and realise that, on departure earlier, I had forgotten to close the window. The bitter cold has permeated the apartment. Sparse, solitary snowflakes float in. It's so pretty I decide to leave it open for a while as I potter around in the kitchen, emptying ashtrays, putting glasses in the sink.

Outside, I hear the doors of the main building creak. Footsteps. I look down and just make out the shape of a person moving slowly across the courtyard.

~

I have a dream about a crowded U-Bahn station. It's peak hour, absolutely packed with people. They're ordinary people, in winter clothes, all waiting for the next train. I realise, at some point, that they're all travelling in pairs. Everyone seems to have a designated partner with them, and they're all completely absorbed in each other, standing on the spot, looking their partners direct in the eye, some holding hands. All the couples are involved in very deep conversations, really connecting on some vital point. The murmuring of many voices makes for one low indecipherable hum. I'm standing in the middle of the platform, listening.

There's someone up ahead of me. I can't see them. But I know I have to follow them. I begin to move through the crowd. The sense of urgency increases. There is someone up ahead and they have something that belongs to me. Something I really need. Whatever they have, they're holding it in their two hands and it is precious and they are getting away. I continue down and down and down along the platform, which never seems to end. I move faster and faster, yelling at people to get out of my way. They can't hear me.

Sitting up in bed now, rubbing the dry skin of my cheeks. All my joints are seized up, my jaw clenched and aching. I must have been grinding my teeth. It's five am. Wide awake but inert in the dark, I know already that this dream is going to cling to me. I'll be carrying its imprint around all day. My nerves are rankled, still holding that sense of urgency, of pursuit.

~

PM. 'Hello? Yes, hello. Hello? Yes, hello, can you hear me? Hello? I'm here, can you hear me? Can you hear me? Hello?' There's a lot of interference.

'Hello.'

'Where have you been?'

'What do you mean? I've been here.' (Your voice is cold, defensive.)

'I've been calling for a week.'

'I haven't felt like talking.'

'I've been calling for a fucking week.'

'Sorry.'

(Silence.)

'What's this about?'

'Look …'

'Why haven't you even responded to my messages?'

'I …'

'Where the fuck have you been?'

'What?'

'This is fucked. I don't want to come home to a shitfight. I want us to talk about this now.'

(I breathe and let my anger settle. I've finally got you on the line and I don't want to lose you.)

'Please, can we talk about it?'

(Please don't go, please don't leave me alone in this silence. Please listen, please listen, please say something.)

'What messages?

'What do you mean, "what messages?"?'

'I didn't get any messages.'

'Bullshit.'

'I didn't.'

(Silence.)

'Hello?'

'Yes, I'm here.'

'Hello?'

'I'm here!'

'My reception's shit. I'm at the farm. Are you there?'

'I'm here!'

'Hello?'

'I'm here!'

(Silence.)

AM. Again, I'm pulled out of sleep too early. Suddenly, violently, I'm pushed to the surface as if through a thick membrane. My chest is tight, creaking like a bellows.

There's a distinct feeling of residual presence. As if someone has just left the room. Traces of hands, of a voice, breath, another body in space. What was I dreaming? What's been interrupted by my waking? I sit up in bed for a while and let forms emerge in the darkness around me. The room takes shape. Everything in its right place. Nobody. Nothing.

I feel propelled out of bed, as if there's some emergency. As if I've woken up late and missed an appointment. Without thinking, I get up and walk through the apartment to the kitchen. It's still dark. I glance at the clock on the wall. Five am. Again. Turn a few circles. Open the fridge. Close it. Open the top drawer. Close it.

There is a feeling, under the gauze of half sleep, of having lost something, needing something. Eventually, I sit, thwarted, at the kitchen table. Stare, calm myself down. Look out the window. Light, beginning very slowly to filter into the atmosphere.

I'm staring out the window for a long time before I notice it: the Hinterhaus. Something about it has changed. It takes me a while to find it. The right-hand side. The second-floor window. There's an object on the sill that wasn't there before – it definitely wasn't there before.

I squint and try to make it out. It looks like a jar. A glass jar. Small, dark – the kind you would use for spices or pills.

You can't access that sill from the ground. Maybe the building is finally being renovated. Maybe there are workmen inside and one of them has left his litter on the windowsill. But I'm curious. I throw on my coat and my boots and head downstairs.

I stare up at it for a while before I decide to dislodge it. I find a long branch on the ground. I rise up onto my toes. My coat rides up and opens as I lift my arms, exposing my flesh to the air. I scrape the tip of the branch along the sill and the jar topples.

It fits in the palm of my hand, but it's heavier than its size would imply. Some kind of old pharmaceutical bottle. Dark glass with a stopper. I shake it and listen.

It's perfectly airtight: the stopper is held fast by a vacuum; it wheezes and pops as I pull it out. A puff of tiny silver particles is released into the air. They coat the throat of the bottle, a few settle on my fingertips.

I can see that there's something in there but I can't make out what. It occurs to me, for the first time, that jars of this nature frequently contain noxious or sensitive substances. I squat on the ground and tentatively invert it, and tap on the base.

A moth. A fat, dead, grey moth falls out onto the ground. I can't know for sure, but my instinct is it was captured alive in there. In its death struggles, its wings have been shredded and the inside of the jar has been coated with silver scales. I look at the particles on my fingers. I pick the moth up and let its dry, furry little body rest in my palm.

I'm overcome by a desire to breathe life back into it. I want so badly to see its wings move. A tickle rises in my throat and breaks into a cough. The force of my breath pushes the moth's body off my palm and on to the ground.

Blueish light, and the electricity of coming snow.

PM. I've heard it so many times now, it doesn't even sound like you.

'Who is this?' you say to me.

'How dare you?' I say to you.

A long silence.

And again: 'Who's there?'

I raise my voice. I shout out to you across this impossible space, through the cold and the dark. From the depths of this underwater city, I'm sending you my last bubbles of air.

Once again: 'Who is this?' You exhale, exasperated, and hang up the phone.

~

I turn the stereo up to full volume.

I want the music to shatter me. I want it to break me open and set the shards rattling, bring out all the broken harmonies. I don't care if the windows crack. I need to bust the seal of this place. If you can't hear me, I'll sing louder. If I can't sing, I'll scream. If I can't scream, I'll dance, kick my feet, flap my wings.

The Triffids again. I set 'My Baby Thinks She's a Train' to repeat. The vibration spreads. Every object sings at a different pitch. The whole room is humming along.

I open my mouth and belt out the chorus. I push my voice out with as much force as I can muster. It hurts. I push harder.

In the dark glass of the kitchen window, I can see my reflection. My mouth is moving. My whole face is straining to give shape to sound. But I can't hear anything of my own voice under the music. There's nothing there. I'm singing as loud as I can and there's nothing. Just tightness, my breath scraping the gutter, a whistle of dry air through the space where my voice should be.

I turn the music off. I lie down on the bed and try to relax, set my whole body to the simple task of drawing breath. In. Out. Follow the rhythm of my inhalations, breathing the silence as if it were an anaesthetic gas. Feeling it spread through my body, counting the seconds backwards.

In.

Out.

Darkness. Settled on top of me, like a heavy blanket.

Washed up on the shore of sleep, bloated and motionless. My

body is so heavy. I feel pulled downwards, into the mattress, as if by the outward movement of the tide. I'm awake. But the life hasn't returned to my limbs. I can feel my whole flesh, alive and suspended in darkness, but I can't move.

I can hear breathing. Heavy, laboured breathing. It's not my breath. My chest is still. I can't feel any movement. I can't feel any air coming in or out. I can't feel my own breath at all. But I can hear another, right up close. Whistling past my ear, coursing down the groove of my neck. The dry, rattling breath of someone close to death.

I can feel my mouth opening. Smoothly and involuntarily, as if by remote control.

Something cold makes contact with my lips and spreads them apart. Something moves over my tongue. It takes me a moment to recognise the sensation and to realise that, yes, at least some part of me is awake.

Long fingers, reaching into my mouth. Hard, cold knuckles. Skin like velum. On it, a mixture of trace odours. Chemical. Organic. Dirt under the fingernails. House smells: the smell of dust, age, mould, damp and dark, filthy cavities. And something else. There's another smell on these fingers: a distinctive base note of pipe tobacco.

I'm gagging violently. I can feel the icy tips moving deeper. My lips stretch over the bridge of the knuckles. I can feel the skin straining and splitting. My jaw suddenly loosens and hinges unnaturally wide. My tongue is being drawn backwards, tearing at the tendon that binds it to the floor of my mouth. That cold hand, fingers gathered to a point, pushes mercilessly deeper into my throat until I can feel the whole thing in there, my teeth almost at the wrist. The nails scrape over the rungs of my trachea.

The fingers have latched onto something in my throat and they're skilfully trying to dislodge it. There's a slight tugging sensation, but no pain. Whatever it is, it separates easily.

The fingers retract, holding something carefully in their grip. It's light, delicate. It's moving. There's a tickle, a fluttering. I feel it scrape softly against my palate as the hand slips out, having broken the elastic of my lips, leaving my jaw slack and capacious.

Suddenly, my ribs expand to full capacity, sucking up a full tank of cold air. Then, from the depths, comes one long, clear note. My voice releases, resounds, fills the room. It continues, steady and strong, drawn from me as if on a string. Then, as my lungs empty, it begins to dissolve into a fragile vibrato. Silence descends, and I'm pulled back down into sleep.

AM. Silver particles in the corners of my mouth. I study them in the bathroom mirror, wipe them off with my fingers.

I splash water on my face. Smear balm over the deep splits in my lips. Get dressed. Lace up my boots and head out into the stairwell.

I cross the courtyard. Pay attention to each step. Each sturdy step across the thickening crust of dirty ice. As always, the smell of smoke. The cold.

At the bakery, the shelves and the refrigerator cabinets have been amply stacked. The bell on the door rings as I enter.

Tobias is nowhere to be seen.

I can hear someone in the kitchen. I think it's them, talking on their phone. Quietly but urgently. They're having a conversation they don't want anyone listening in on, but their voice raises irrepressibly at certain points. I can make out fragments: I can hear them repeating the words, *Ich liebe dich. Ich liebe dich.* Over and over again, like a spell. *Ich liebe dich. Ich liebe dich.* Their voice is weak and slurred, and I think they're crying.

Through the lens of the shop window, I see the shape of a person, indistinct in its padded layers, waddle into frame. The figure enters the shop, peels back the hood of its anorak and reveals itself as a young woman. She walks straight into the kitchen, nearly tripping over something – the sniffling goth, Tobias, who's slouched on the floor near the door.

They don't bother with shift-changeover pleasantries. The woman goes about her business. Tobias stands up, pinches their nose between their fingers, and stands in frozen profile in the doorway for a moment. Pulls off their white smock and flings it into a basket under a bench. Without a word, they gather themself and their belongings and walk out.

They pause for a moment on the street to light a cigarette. Cast a glance back through the glass. Their eye make-up has spread through their crow's-feet and across the bridge of their nose. Their proud mouth twitches slightly. Then, with an exhalation of smoke and a flick of red hair, they're gone.

I take my seat. Wait.

Unspeakable.

I T BEGINS WITH A fence, because this is a city of perimeters. It begins with me walking, walking alongside the wire, walking in the late afternoon, in the autumn half-light. Walking with my eyes closed and my arms crossed, walking and swerving, with a hangover, nauseous, shaking, inappropriately dressed, freezing but sweating toxins, walking and wishing already that I wasn't there.

Walking, and panicking a little that maybe this is futile anyway, that I'm too late, that I shouldn't have stayed out last night knowing that I had to make this trip, knowing that this box had to be ticked today, walking and wondering where I am, following the fence, trusting the fence, hoping that somewhere along it an entrance point will appear.

There are hulking soviet apartment blocks. There is washing on balconies. There is a mother and daughter, dressed in identical white hooded anoraks, tightly fitted, waiting at the bus stop. There are dudes in tracksuits with pit bulls. There are endless driveways, but no cars. There are works in progress, new residential developments going up, construction noises, billboards with floorplans and artists' impressions of new kitchens, new bathrooms, new living spaces.

Alongside the things to come, the things that are. The things that have been here for a long time, next to the thing – *the* thing – that cannot be incorporated into the new, *the* thing that everyone comes here to see, *the* thing that, while not the geographical centre of town, nonetheless forms it nucleus.

Other cities open on to market squares. They move inward from the outskirts toward a central space that is shared, open: claimed and inhabited by everyone. But this city, this small city, about two hours from the old capital by bus, is built around an enclosure. What is fenced out exists in relation to what is fenced in: they look each other in the face, daily, with dull recognition. Uninterested, they observe the flow of outsiders. Millions of them. Every year. This point is marked in bold on any tourist's map of the eastern states: it is not only the centre of town, but was once, by a certain system of logic, the designated centre of Europe.

This city has two names. There is the name of the actual location, the Polish name: the name on the window of the bus that gets you here, and on the police station and the post office. This name, Oświęcim, belongs to the people who live here. Who have always lived here. The town has another, better-known name, a Germanised version inherited from an occupying force. It's this name that is familiar and spoken everywhere, a shorthand reference to monumental horror. It hangs in heavy black lettering, as much a graphic representation of an idea as a word. More than half a century after the invasion, this town remains occupied territory:

it is occupied by the living, who co-exist with the multitudinous dead. It is occupied by its own irreducible significance as a site of pilgrimage, the property of world history. It is fully occupied by history, as an empty room is fully occupied by emptiness.

I can't find the entrance. I crouch down and consider a cigarette, because smoking is what you do when you're lost or waiting. I was out until breakfast, drinking with a nineteen-year-old millionaire from Warsaw. I had been at a bar in Kazimierz after a gig with some friends, and this dude and his retinue descended on our table for no obvious reason other than to extend largesse and command our attention. He had two bodyguards in tow, one for personal protection and one to ferry trays of shots between the bar and our table. This is, surely, the pinnacle of tourist kitsch: I found the vodka, and now I have to find the death camp. I get up and keep walking, keep following the fence.

Eventually I come to a gate. I make my way through the parking lot towards the main building. It's squat and featureless. A few shrubs and a rock wall, a gesture to the niceties of landscaping. I can't see any people. Anywhere. There are a couple of cars parked outside though. And through the glass doors at the entrance, I can see a light on.

It's almost five. I half expect the doors to already be locked, so I push on them gingerly. To my surprise, they open, and I find myself in a long corridor. Green lino. Fluorescent light. It's like a hospital. I stand at the entrance for a few moments. I become aware of a low murmuring of voices, coming from somewhere deeper in the building. I move off in search of the ticketing booth, and discover it at the end of the hall.

Behind the glass are three attendants, all women in their sixties, identically dressed in grey V-necks, all sporting silver blow-waves and spectacles on chains. They're chatting to each other, emptying tills, punching numbers into EFTPOS machines, counting notes with rubber-tipped fingers. It's looking suspiciously like the end of the day. I'm standing at the counter for a while before one of them notices me. She looks at me for a long time, silently, with an expression of complete disinterest that mutates into contempt.

'I want to buy a ticket,' I tell her.

She shakes her head briskly. 'The museum is closed.'

There's a frustrated exchange.

'The guidebook told me seven pm,' I say.

'In the summertime only,' she replies.

'I've come from Krakow,' I say.

'You can go in on your own, if you like,' she says, and I think she's being sarcastic, but she's not. 'You can go in on your own and you'll have to find a security guard to let you out. Though it's getting dark and you might not be able to find your way around without someone who knows the compound, and many of the exhibits will be locked. It's your choice,' she says.

I stare at the floor and consider my options.

I hear footsteps approach from behind, a pair of sensible boots on a mission, moving decidedly in the direction of the door. The woman serving me looks up, over my shoulder, and gestures for me to turn around. There's a man passing, carrying a backpack, an empty lunch box and other remnants of a working day. He goes to wave goodbye to the attendants but halts when he sees me.

'Here is your solution,' says the attendant. 'A private guide. He will cost you two hundred zloty.'

He approaches the counter. Looks at me, looks at the attendant and there is a brief exchange between them in Polish, which I can assume goes something along the lines of: do you mind, I know it's been a long day, but this fuckwit has come all this way and they need someone to show them around. He nods and smiles, and in that moment I'm very grateful for that smile.

He's young, maybe thirty. Very tall, and awkwardly aware of it. He stoops to introduce himself, extending his hand. Pale eyes, blond, with a short fringe crowning a high forehead. Khaki parka. He introduces himself as Wojciech. He stuffs his lunchbox back in his bag, fumbles his beanie back onto his head and says, 'We better get going.'

He explains the situation. This is the main compound. Birkenau is a ten-minute drive down the road. If I want to see it, we have to get in his car and go now.

'There's no electricity out there,' he says. 'We have to catch it while there's still some light.'

He leads me out to the parking lot and we jump into his white hatchback and tear off down the road. It's a long, narrow road, across a plain. It carves an uncompromisingly straight trajectory through emptiness towards one point. It's a new road, built to connect the two sites, laid parallel to its shadow, which Wojciech points out to my right: the old train line, the dark rails still intact but sinking gradually into the pale grass. This was the main transport line. I think about this word: *transport*.

And there it is: the brick watchtower, the fence and the lamps bowing their massive heads down towards the ground, but issuing no light. Suddenly we're in a colour reproduction of something that should be black and white. We are in a photograph; we are on the set of a film that has been made and remade many times.

Memorial and evidence are, of course, not the same thing. If evidence is comprised of objective physical remnants (a matter of what *is*) then memorial occupies a different space. At first sight, evidence is dumb. It is a building, sitting in a field. It's smaller than you imagined it would be. There is no accompanying soundtrack; it is not part of any cohesive narrative. The connection is delayed, the symbolic fails, the engine of affect stalls. Given the right circumstances, this will change: the field of memorial is a vast one, with many master architects in its employ. The means and methods of constructing a memorial may be as varied as the events that warrant memorialising, but the basic principle remains the same: evidence and memorial (site and narrative) exist in relation to each other as the train tracks do: parallel, never meeting, but working in confluence to bring us to one point. That point: evidence plus memorial equals *monument*.

We park, and make our way in. We pass through the archway and step out onto uneven ground, sloping down towards the first row of wooden barracks. There's an expanse of healthy-looking grass, with networks of paths trodden into it. Urban planners have a name for these lines, a beautiful one: *desire lines*. So-called because they mark out the shortest route between one point and another, in this case the archway and the row of barracks. These paths have been worn in by visitors. Originally, there would have just been mud and ice. No system for foot traffic, no clear path for entrance or exit.

'There would have been no grass here,' Wojciech tells me. 'People would have eaten it.'

Maybe he always starts with the grass. Maybe this is always first on his practised litany of details.

He leads me into the first of the buildings. It's like a stable; the walls are not walls but rows of planks, shoddily hammered together. There are outlines, which gradually take the shape of objects and structures: rows of reconstructed bunks, of stone squat toilets. Everything exists in rows, in brutal uniformity. He shows me around, rattling off his script at speed, with the flair of an estate agent showing off a grand home to an interested client.

He identifies the main features but laces his description with finer points, points of humanity, points to bring this massive thing into focus. He uses just enough poetic licence to bring the dates, statistics, big numbers, to life. His perhaps the only licensed poetic, or sanctioned poetic, of the experience of which he is the officiator. In this light I can't read any of the information panels, so I rely entirely on his verbal record, which just keeps rolling, as if he's got it on tape.

When we step out of the barracks it's almost completely dark. The ground, the buildings, the path: it has all become indistinguishable from the settling night. There are two points of orientation: to the north, the watchtower, a contained hub of electric light; to the south, a forest of shadows, the outline of a thick woodland at the farthest perimeter, cut out against the sky.

The sunsets of central Europe, at this time of year, are strange. So orange, such a fiery apricot, not unlike the colour of an Australian sky in bushfire season, but cold. Everything below the silhouette of the trees, by contrast, has sunk into black. This gives the impression, for a moment, that we are suspended at the mouth of a vast pit. The ground, the invisible ground, is what stops us from falling.

We stand at the mouth of the main line that divides the two halves of the camp: the central passage, the backbone of the compound.

Wojciech gestures into the darkness, pointing out faintly visible shapes. 'Down there is the Judenrampe, where human cargo, in inconceivable quantities, was efficiently offloaded and sorted, individuals assessed and marked for labour or for death. Beyond that is the site where the two main crematoria stood before they were frantically destroyed by the SS in the days leading up to liberation.'

There are warehouses, the colloquially named Canada A and Canada B, so-called because they were 'places of plenty', where the possessions of prisoners were sent for sorting before being repurposed or redistributed on the open market. But it's dark and neither of us can see these things, not so much as an outline. They're vast images, projected into vast darkness.

I'm standing there for a while before I realise that I am alone. Wojciech has already turned and made it halfway back up the hill.

'We have to leave now,' he calls to me, walking quickly in the direction of the gate.

The archway is illuminated by the accidental light cast from an open door. As we get closer I look in: fluoros and buzzing security monitors broadcasting different shades of night-vision green. In this world, things are seen in reverse: the black buildings become grainy white, the brittle trace of a fence visible against a dark background.

There's light grey carpet and formica benchtops. I can smell instant coffee and vinyl and damp wool carpet. Under the parapet of the iconic archway, the frozen mouth of Birkenau, there's an office. It smells and sounds like every other office on the planet.

There's a group of guards inside, about five of them, milling around or sitting with their booted feet up on the tables, talking and laughing. They're wearing the generic uniform of state authority: navy blue V-necks, boots, shaved heads, utility belts. They could be bored transit cops at a suburban railway station.

Wojciech is walking ahead of me. He pauses for a beat at the door. When he sees the guards, he flinches. Utters a nervous, 'Cześć.'

The guards look at us. They say nothing. One of them smiles. A smile that's spiked with something, a bully's smile. The man holds Wojciech's gaze silently. Then turns to me. His grin widens.

'Come,' Wojciech urges, before moving off, quickening his pace, dragging me away as a mother might drag a small child from the sight of something lurid.

We walk over the icy road in the direction of the white hatchback. We can see it, parked fifty metres or so down the road. Wojciech is walking briskly. A little too briskly. He seems overly keen to get away from this place and into the safety of his car. I worry that if I don't get there in time he'll just jump in and speed off. I'm struggling to keep up. I can hear his breath. I can see it, issuing from his mouth in an urgent plume, like steam from a locomotive.

There is, in this moment, a very real sense of being pursued by something shapeless and immeasurably threatening. We are both working hard, over this short distance, to suppress the creeping tremor of panic, to keep walking quickly but calmly in the direction of the car and, most importantly, not give in to the impulse to break into a run. Or, conversely, to stop entirely, turn around, and look back.

We make it to the car, and Wojciech's veneer of professional composure is teetering. He jams the key in the lock, wrenches the door open. We get in. Wojciech slams and locks his door, and reaches across me to lock mine. He grips the steering wheel with both hands. He's shaking. His eyes are closed, he's breathing heavily through his nose. He has retreated from his well-oiled performance as museum guide and sole protector of a bewildered tourist, into a private negotiation with his own fear.

I wonder for a second about the specifics of this fear. What is its substance, its form?

'I hate coming here at night,' he says. 'I hate it. I got stuck out here once. On All Souls night. The car broke down. There is no mobile reception. I had to sleep all night in the back seat.'

He starts the engine. The dashboard lights up.

He says, 'I could not sleep. All night I felt outside there were people. Watching through the windows. People trying to get in.'

We have shifted again to the exterior shot of the Birkenau watchtower. The greater outline of the building is invisible. What we see is a small hub of light, contained by the archway, suspended in darkness without limits. And within it, the figures of five men. Arms folded, watching us as we pull away.

It begins, again, with a fence. A fence within a fence, and another open gate. Another iconic entrance point, crowned with scrolling iron fretwork, following a decorative curve. From the inside, the German words *Arbeit Macht Frei* read in reverse.

Beneath the famous declaration, there's another sign, nailed to a stake at eye-level. A picture of an ice-cream cone, of all things. With a big red line through it.

An acquaintance in Berlin had told me to look out for this. Ice creams prohibited. *Who the fuck*, he had asked me, *would want to walk around Auschwitz eating a fucking ice cream?* The person in question happened to be a white Australian, and I remember answering him: *Do you know how many times I've declined invitations from white friends to camp or picnic on a massacre site? Do you understand the first thing about where you come from?*

The first stop on the tour of the main compound is the gas chamber. The bunker-like structure is humped under a mound of turf, like a shoebox under a rug. It's not more than one hundred metres from the first row of barracks that would have housed prisoners. The same distance away, in the other direction, beyond the wire fence, is an apartment block. The face of the building is made up of a tessellation of small windows. Some of them you can see straight through. Others are covered by curtains. Through one, the ghostly flickering of a television and, through another, the cut-out shape of a fern in a hanging basket. Through another, someone's fridge door, covered in magnets and photos. Somebody just turned their balcony light on.

Passing through the low door into the chamber the first thing I do, the first thing I believe most people do, is vividly imagine my own death. I'm struck by the predictability of this reaction, as well as its obscenity.

I stay inside for a long time. Wojciech hovers near the door, silent for the most part. He jumps in every now and then with a statistic or a description, something I should know, something about the pope's visit, or something about the twin incinerators (which are reproductions), decorated with wreaths and burnt-out Yahrzeit candles. But, mostly, he leaves me to my own devices.

The eye is drawn to detail. It is unable to bring more than one object, or even more than one point on an object, into focus at the same time. I notice the pipes. Chips in the paintwork. Condensation on the roof. Shadows and electric light. I stare for a moment right into the glowing tungsten of the bulb in the ceiling, let it burn into my retina. Then close my eyes: the glowing imprint floats there, on the surface of darkness, like a leaf in water.

What the eye clearly sees is minuscule relative to what the eye is peripherally aware of. The eye will be drawn to things that correspond to its own size and shape, just as the body will be drawn to another body, and the heart will be drawn to another heart, again, of familiar substance and dimensions. It's not that numbers are cold. Eleven million is not a cold number. But there are certain processes of connection and understanding that must initially happen on a human scale. You have to take them first, on some level, into your own body. Why else would anyone feel the need to visit such a place in the flesh? Why else this necessity to view the *evidence*? Does an oral account of a massacre hold less weight? The answer is no, it doesn't. Not to the one doing the telling. Not to the body that holds a blood-memory of that story. But I wonder about the differential mechanisms of remembering. Or purposeful forgetting, as the case may be.

I don't know how to name this particular process of projected identification. The first death I imagine, when I enter this space, is my own. My own body is the first body. The second body is Wojciech's, and his is the second death. Only after those two can I begin to extend my understanding to the idea of a blurry multitude. And even in the smoke, I'm trying to make out their faces, trying to give them names and occupations and families, imagining the anomalies of their naked bodies, crowded into this room, the size of their feet or their hips, how strange or how familiar they might have been to each other.

'It's quite pleasant in the summertime,' Wojciech tells me.

After pointing out a patch of grass in between the chamber and the Kommandant's residence, and telling me that this is the place where a gallows once stood, he adds that it's also the spot where, when the weather is nice, he likes to have his lunch. It's true that compared to the wild expanse of Birkenau, Auschwitz, with its arcades of plane trees and old brick buildings, is almost cosy.

Wojciech slips much more casually out of his tour-guide register now.

As we walk he complains about the unevenness of the ground. 'This museum gets more money than any other museum in the country,' he says, 'and they can't even fix the footpaths.'

I have the feeling of being drawn into his confidence, and there's comfort in this. There's fascination too. There's a peculiar sense of after-hours intimacy. We have mutually entrusted ourselves to each other. We are both so glad to have someone. At this moment in time and in this place, neither of us wants to be alone.

I agree with him, the ground is very uneven.

'It's a menace!' he insists. He tells me that once he had an elderly lady on his tour who tripped and split her knee open. He had to take her to the infirmary, another guide had to take over the tour, it was a huge drama. He sat with the woman as they fixed her up. 'I nearly fainted,' he tells me. 'I can't stand blood or the smell of bandages. And she was so old. Her bones, bones so old, they just snap.'

Inside, Wojciech has to fumble for the light switch. In the darkness my hand touches a cold railing. A little bit sticky, like it's been freshly painted.

The lights flicker on. We're in a stairwell.

I'm assailed by odd details. We walk up a flight of steps that leads to the museum and the archives. We come to a room full of maps and documents. There is a large map of Europe, which takes up a whole wall. The land mass is painted salmon pink, crossed by a network of taut wires, strung between nails. A nail hammered in at Dachau, another at Buchenwald etc. The lines between them represent the transit passages. Auschwitz–Birkenau is right at the centre. Here, everything converges.

If this was a convex trajectory, we would be standing at the vanishing point. Of all things, I'm reminded of an image from a cartoon. An episode of *Danger Mouse* that I watched as a kid. Danger Mouse and Penfold get sucked into a black hole. Except it wasn't a *black* hole, it was salmon pink. With swirling lines, sucked inexorably downward, to one point.

This is the first of many unrelated and occasionally absurd images and memories of my own that arises. Flotsam and jetsam from my childhood for the most part, continually floating to the surface of my mind with each new piece of information that the exhibit offers up. In the faces of the multitudinous dead, I can't help but see people I know.

When we enter the infamous room full of human hair, I single out a lone black plait in the mass. I'm reminded of the dismembered braid that my mother keeps in a drawer at home. (I cut it off at fifteen – she wept.) I think of the spiritual amputation suffered by Native children in residential schools – the cutting of braids, the severance of culture. I think of all the Indigenous hair that sits in museum basements, tagged and numbered, along with our bones. I stare at the glass case full of spectacles, and my eyes are drawn to a pair that look exactly like those worn by a friend.

I wonder what this is achieving, if there is a kind of narcissism inherent in any process of understanding. Familiar images, entirely banal in their nature, are chosen at random. These images hustle and assemble, it seems, to aid the assimilation of a horror of such a scale. Horror, as a filmic or literary genre, relies on familiar settings to achieve its effect. Perhaps true horror, the horror of atrocity and its remnants, relies on the same, if it is to be viscerally understood. If horror is a genre in which a thrill is elicited by a making-strange of the familiar, then perhaps museums of atrocity reverse this process: the unimaginable is made personable through the endless accumulation of fine detail.

Spectacles, shoes, suitcases, gloves, hair. All of these things were stripped from prisoners on their arrival, then sorted in the Canada warehouses. I wonder why they kept the hair. Did they use it to stuff mattresses? Did they sell it to wigmakers? The phrase *dumber than a box of hair* asserts itself into my thoughts and, for a second, I almost laugh. Like the shoes and everything else, the thing that haunts me most about these objects is not what has been collected, but what has been dispersed. The belongings of the dead were processed and sold on. They were a source of capital for a resource-hungry regime. A regime that was deeply concerned with appealing to the perverse morals of Bavarian Protestantism: *waste not, want not.*

I'm reminded of a bucket of leather gloves at a second-hand store in Kreuzberg. I picked out a pair for myself and a pair for a lover. They would have been about the same vintage: 1930s, 1940s. There were hundreds of them. Like limp fish in a barrel. How do you account for the provenance of everyday things? Does atrocity spread, like an insidious and invisible fungus, into the tiniest cracks of the ordinary? How long does it hang around for, and how does it mutate?

The question persists: why did they keep the hair? There was a purpose for this – I remember Wojciech telling me what it was. And I remember another conversation that I had with a colleague, a Kurdish artist who makes large-scale sculptures from human hair. *Nothing will live in it,* she told me. *Nothing. Once it's cropped from the scalp, it's the deadest thing you can imagine.* She said, *I have clumps of it in my garden. No animal touches it, not insects or birds. Nothing will build a nest out of it. It's like it's cursed.*

I remember telling her that I was brought up to never leave hair behind in a brush, to sweep up carefully after trimming my fringe.

This is the final exhibit: a series of empty rooms. In the basement of the barracks, which houses the museum, there's a labyrinthine complex of cells. Again, as we descend, the first thing I'm reminded of is something from my childhood: the sinister crawl space underneath a house I lived in, and my older brother play-threatening to lock me down there. This memory comes to me with its edges sanded off, blurred with dreams and other realities. What lingers is not an image but a sense, a recognition of the subterranean as something fearful. It is, it seems, the earliest part of me that connects with this fear. Barely suppressed beneath the sensible adult, there is the raw panic of a very young child.

There is a long corridor illuminated by naked bulbs. Like the bronchi that feed each lung, the core pipeline spiders off into ever-diminishing passageways lined with cells. The cells range from the size of a bedroom to the size of a closet. These ones, the small ones, are *starvation cells*, a vertical version of the oubliette (Fr. *oublier*, to forget), which is to be found beneath the dungeon floor of most medieval castles throughout Europe and the UK. I saw one of these, too, on a trip to Warwick Castle when I was ten.

It's a medieval idea, medievally barbaric, that stands out against the hyper-modern, mass-industrialised barbarism that generally distinguishes the Third Reich from other genocidal machines. In each cell there is standing room for a single prisoner, who would be sealed in there without food or water, and left to die on their feet. Even in the denigrated, half-starved state in which most prisoners would have made it into these cells, death by starvation is still a lengthy process. It's weeks, in most cases, before the body begins to devour itself.

This is one of many contradictory answers to the assertion of the Reich's supposed *efficiency*. That quality which German society continues to pride itself on. I've spent enough time living in Germany to know that this cultural myth is just that: a myth. The Nazis were just as sloppy and gleefully cruel as any other genocidal machine.

The walls are greenish. They are covered with scratches. What looks from a distance like a frenzied scramble of marks reveals itself at closer inspection to be incredibly detailed graffiti. It's predominantly religious in motif, and every major faith of Europe appears to be represented, as well as every language. Polish Catholics, with their particularly developed grasp of the aesthetics of iconography, are the most visible on these particular walls.

It's when I focus on an elaborately carved image of the crucifixion that – for the first time on this strange, numb journey – I feel completely overcome. In its presence (and this image is a presence, beyond representation) something connects. It is the heart-sized object. On the wall of a starvation cell, it's so passionately, intricately, and sensitively carved. It's not the religiosity of the image that moves me, nor even the circumstances of its production, but its artistry. Its beauty.

Wojciech has removed his beanie and is kneading it with both hands as he speaks. He tells me that it was in this basement that the Nazis first began experimenting with Zyklon B. This was not a specially engineered chemical weapon but a readily available industrial pesticide, used in factories to kill vermin. It could be bought cheaply in bulk.

Upstairs in the museum, there is a cabinet containing a pile of empty cans. The labels are peeling and age-spotted, with blue lettering. It doesn't look like an instrument of mass murder. It didn't come in massive, unlabelled drums. It came in tins with labels and snappy typography. You could buy it off the shelf.

The first control group were largely sick and disabled people, the elderly, and children. About two hundred people were confined in this basement. Wojciech gestures to the row of grates near the ceiling: he tells me they were sealed, making the basement 'hermetic', to use his choice of words.

The gas was filtered in, in different concentrations. At first, it was too weak. The back of the box indicated the amounts required for killing rats. They had vastly underestimated how much they would need. It took the prisoners two days to die.

He's saying this and, suddenly, he's interrupted by the sound of laughter. Muffled laughter, coming to us, it seems, from no particular direction. We look at each other. We hear the door slam shut. The heavy bolt slide into place.

Wojciech bolts up the stairs. I'm staring at the outline of my frozen shadow on the concrete floor, my heart thumping, a constriction in my throat. He's screaming in Polish and hammering the door. The sound of his voice rebounds off the walls, and multiplies. Suddenly the room is filled with screaming, with a host of voices.

For a moment I'm glued to the spot. Then, my body chooses flight. I run up the stairs after my guide, feeling like there's something clinging to me, pulling me backwards.

The bolt slides away and the door opens. There's a security guard standing there. Grinning. He laughs raucously. Slaps the terrified Wojciech on the shoulder. What a good joke.

Wojciech's knuckles are still clenched and look raw from banging. I see the red in his eyes, the tears on his face. The string of spit hanging from his mouth. His breath.

~

He walks me to his car.

'You're very brave coming out here, alone in the dark like this,' he says. 'I mean, it's not Disneyland.'

'It wasn't my intention,' I say. 'Just bad planning.'

Wojciech wants to leave. He tells me he wants a job in a city museum. Something in archiving or preservation, something out of the public eye. He'd like to spend his days immersed in a less hostile history. Handling quiet objects in quiet halls – things that take nothing from you and leave no residue.

His girlfriend is restless too. She works as a receptionist in a sports club. But she, like Wojciech, is a historian by vocation. They both hate Oświęcim. They're doing time here, until something else comes along.

'It's particularly hard for her,' he tells me. 'She's not Polish. She doesn't speak the language very well, has difficulty making friends.'

I ask him where she's from, and he says: she's German.

We arrive at the bus station, which is a space-age construction, fresh out of the plastic, on the outskirts of town. It's lit up like an aquarium and totally empty. The screens inside are all blacked out. Wojciech doesn't know when – or if – a bus will arrive to take me back to Krakow.

He waits with me in the cold on the side of the road for a bus that may or may not arrive. He talks about England. He spent six months travelling there. He loved it; he hitchhiked everywhere, improved his English chatting to lorry drivers. He asks me where I live and I tell him mostly London at the moment but I move around a lot.

Wojciech and his girlfriend want to move. Maybe to London. Maybe to Berlin. They met in Berlin, and she misses it. As a city, Wojciech likes it a lot. There's good music. Good falafel. Some of the best museums in Europe. 'But London is so exciting,' he says. 'London is an engine.'

We spend almost an hour like this. Talking in circles, talking a fence around what has gone before, sealing it off.

When a battered transit van approaches, Wojciech flags it down. There's a scrawled cardboard sign reading *KRAKOW* propped in the front window. The door slides open: inside, the radio is croaking out the hit parade, the driver is smoking, the passengers are talking, each in their own language – Polish, German, French, Spanish – a simmering potlatch where a strand of one becomes entangled with another. There's room for one more passenger.

I shake Wojciech's hand and thank him.

Playback.

MY NIGHTS ARE DEEP and soundless. I've stopped dreaming.

Every morning, there's a moment, suspended in that grey space between sleep and waking, in which there is no sensation. I'm just a body: a set of lungs and a heart that beats easily.

Every morning, sunlight splits the drapes. Every morning, the birds. Every morning, I set my feet into the thick carpet next to my bed and hold them there, anchoring myself. I walk to the kitchen, into that golden light. The water. I can't see it, but I can feel its cool proximity. I can smell the brine rising.

I sit on the blue sofa in the sunroom, with my eyes closed and the window open, listening to the currawongs, the morning rumbles of the estuary, the splutter of small engines.

The currawongs, the river traffic; these are my bone songs. My home frequencies. These are the sounds that have held me since I was born and have never failed, before now, to sing me back into this ground that grew me up.

This time, this homecoming, there's a signal failure. Not dissonance. Not interference. A vacuum where a familiar resonance should be.

This place is named for the meeting of saltwater and fresh. It sits at the tip of a crooked phalanx of land that separates the river from the sea. I landed on a Tuesday, midday. I shelled out for a taxi. It's a long drive from the airport, more than an hour along the coastal road when it's choked with summer traffic. I remember the journey that bright morning of my arrival: crumpled in the back seat, swollen and gritty after thirty hours in the air. Acrid breath of molten bitumen, hot vinyl clinging to the backs of my arms. The radio and the sunlight and everything else turned up too high, too loud.

It had been a long time since I'd travelled that stretch of road. A decade, nearly. Every detail was searing. I remember rounding the bend at the top of the south headland. The clench in my heart at the sight of the ocean. The swell was huge that day, signs planted in the sand: *BEACH CLOSED*. Days before I flew out, the whole coast had been pummelled by heavy storms. This part had been spared the worst of it, but further north the tide had been rough enough to wash a Russian coal ship onto the beach. I'd seen pictures in the news before I left and shown them to Elke. *Can you believe this shit?* The massive red hull, wedged into the sand. *That's about an hour's drive from where we're going.*

As the taxi rounded every crook in the old road I took an inventory of what was still there, and what was not. I recall a scattered assemblage, sights and sensations piling up. Saltbush. Cicadas. The hairpin turn at the top of the headland, the sudden, bilious descent into town. Town being: two intersecting streets and a sleepy cluster of shopfronts. Rounding the final bend in the road, the sudden revelation of the estuary. A silvery expanse of flat water, small craft in their moorings, that little strip of sand, the ferry wharf.

The tide was out when I passed by that morning, exposing the pylons, densely adorned with kelp and oyster shells. That ashen strip of sand, strewn with post-storm debris. A pack of boys, maybe in their early teens, slouched against the railing, arms folded against their bare brown torsos. A pelican on a lamp post, incongruously large and perfectly still.

The Video Ezy was gone; the bakery, still there. The bowlo and the arcade and the chicken shop, all still there. The newsagency, gone. The local primary school, a cluster of demountables on a block of balding grass, still there, shuttered up for the holidays. The big bloodwood tree, the one that stood at the corner of Caulfield Road and Lyme Street. The tree that bled rubies. That was gone.

86 Caulfield Road: still there. As it always had been and as I knew it would be. The same glowering, heavy-set windows and the same crumbling plasterwork. The same three cars parked out the front. As the taxi rolled past I peered through the foliage to the dark glass of the kitchen window; for a moment I thought I made out the fleeting shape of a person. A smudge of black hair, a trail of smoke. I thought about asking the driver to stop.

A block or so past 86, Caulfield Road inclines sharply and ascends, via an arcade of redgums, eventually doglegging into a cul-de-sac, Terrania Crescent. The last street, the end of town. A row of big houses behind high walls.

This town has always been home to strange polarities. The flat, dusty-guttered streets around town and leading to the beach, that's one world. That's the world that I knew as a child. Up here on the hill is a different story: Terrania Crescent is home to a discrete cluster of mansions behind high walls. Built before there was really a town, before there was even a road in or out of the place. All of the houses on the hill have private moorings, left over from a time when this part of the coast was only accessible by boat. The perfect spot to build a retreat as a prewar ruling-class bohemian. Lots of old, white, eccentric money, and at least one dissipated former recording artist.

Beyond that brace of big houses, thick scrub guards the sheer precipice down to the estuary, with its tea-dark waters and circling bull sharks. The trees there rain cicada shells in the right season – we used to go up there to collect them. I remember my cousins – Jack and Ngaire – running ahead of me, scab-kneed and feral, all the way to the top of the hill. We'd find different points of access to the inscrutable snare of brush that hummed with wild sounds.

The key was where the landlord said it would be. I don't think I even caught his name. I gathered from our exchanges, via the housesitting website where I had found the listing, that he was maybe a lawyer or a trustee of the property rather than its primary resident. He offered six weeks of accommodation in exchange for light maintenance and gardening, as well as the care and feeding of Lulu: an ancient, striped tabby cat.

I set my bags down and wandered through the hushed expanse of rooms. I walked around for who knows how long, looking for a place to put myself. I threw open the drapes as I went, sunlight flooding in, illuminating the interior, cut-glass trinketry sending sprays of amber light across the walls. There was a faint but pervasive smell: a base of dark alcohol and smoke, notes of musty floral resting on something else – dank, indolent – which I couldn't place.

The house is a monument to late Deco: all tiered cream curves. Downstairs: a long hallway, and a suite of two rooms off the right side, which I would claim as my own. At the end, a bright kitchen and sunroom. An old television and a landline phone. A blue sofa and a view of the back patio. To the left, a formal lounge and dining room, in a state of partial dissolution: furniture removed or covered, tea chests half filled with packing beads, stacks of books and magazines, all the interstitial stuff of someone's life – broken bits of unidentified medical equipment, old pens and postcards, half-finished tissue boxes, battered tins and jars of buttons.

The upper level is accessed via a sweeping arc of stairs, a gracious ascent. Upstairs, I found the remains of a bedroom. Twin beds, stripped of their linens. I opened the closet to discover it still hung with well-pressed woollen garments, a few pairs of polished brogues, lined up with their toes pushed together.

A hallway leads onwards from the master bedroom to an informal sort of sitting room, with a view of the garden. In there: a sturdy armchair, upholstered in salmon brocade. A table beside it, brown liquor in crystal decanters, and two upturned glasses. A deck of cards, poised on the corner, as if they had been left there mid-game. Old ones, their edges gone fuzzy from handling. Set into the bay window, a mossy green chaise longue, bathed in a bolt of sunlight.

That room leads, finally, to another. Separated by a set of French doors. A room which, on first assessment, was totally empty. Nothing but a large, round rug on the floor, forest green and fringed. I stood in the half-darkness for a long moment, before I heard a soft rasp from behind me. I turned around, scanned the shadows.

Eventually, in the far corner, I made out a dense patch of dark static, cat-shaped.

'This must be Lulu,' I sing-songed, lowering myself to the ground, clicking my tongue. 'Lulu.'

She didn't move. Narrowed her eyes.

My things, all in their places. My suitcase, spilling its contents in the corner. All my gear – sequencers, pedals, my computer, looped cables and jacks of different sizes – laid out on the desk by the window, ready for work. A handful of loose euros, crumpled receipts and other refuse from my pockets, scattered on the nightstand. This room, my room: dark and cool. Olive green wallpaper. Threadbare carpet. On really hot days, the air condenses. By midafternoon, the walls are moist as skin. There's a hulking bureau, its drawers stuffed with someone else's lifetime of disordered paperwork. Smudges on the walls where pictures used to be. The single daybed in the corner and a solid mahogany desk, directly opposite the room's one window. It looks out on to a sandstone terrace, fringed by agapanthus.

I arrived here with a plan. This plan involved two people.

It was going to go like this: I would fly out first, and Elke would follow me a week later. I booked and paid for the tickets with the cash from my last job. I would scoop her up from the airport, and we would take the same journey I took to get here, up the coast road. I would bore her by pointing out every landmark: the beach, the jetty, the bowlo, the bloodwood tree, or what was left of it. Marta's house. All these things would have a story, a texture. I'd hoped Elke might learn to love these waters as I do. We'd swim, and stretch our salted skins out in the sun.

Most importantly, the person I sort of called my lover would meet the person I sort of called my mother and see the place I sort of called my hometown. We would head over to 86 Caulfield Road with a bag of fresh fish and cook it up with Marta and Ross and the cousins, and we'd eat it on the front step under the she-oaks, and Marta would make Elke laugh. We would retire to our mansion on the hill, which I had proudly scored for our temporary home, and we would get to work. I had half our equipment; she'd bring the rest. A month or so was what we needed, to finish what we started. A month or so, somewhere far away.

We made plans. We laid them carefully, knowing that this might be our last chance.

She asked me again and again: *How long is the flight?*

I said, again and again: *It depends. Between twenty-four and thirty hours, depending on the transit times.*

Distances and temporalities of this magnitude are something Antipodeans tend to take for granted – at least, those of us who choose, or are compelled, to live our lives in transit. I can recall periods of my working life when I've made the journey between Australia and Europe six, eight or ten times in a year. To most Europeans this is inconceivable. Elke had refused to believe me when I told her that in the southern hemisphere, the water drains counterclockwise.

I remember that first day, stripping off layer after clammy layer of clothing, and putting myself under a cool stream of water. Letting the journey sluice off me. I thought about Elke, where she was now, and how it would be when she arrived. I stood in the shower, feet planted, and I made plans. Watched streams of soap spiralling down the plughole, imagining her amazement.

It had been snowing heavily when I left. She drove me to the airport. We embraced each other in our heavy winter jackets.

I said: *Maybe you could take mine home for me? I won't need it.*

She was reluctant. She said: *I'll see you soon.*

When I first got here, I left that coat slumped over a chair by the door. It's still there. I can't bring myself to touch it.

I had written to her when I arrived. Let her know that I had landed safely, told her a bit about the house. I told her about the currawongs, told her that I didn't know how much I'd missed their song until I heard it again. I told her they had cut down the bloodwood tree. I asked her to confirm her flight details for me, so I could arrange to come get her. Maybe I could borrow Marta's car.

The days passed without response. Strange mornings in a strange house. Strange mornings, sitting on a stranger's sofa and feeding a stranger's cat, drinking bitter grounds from a stranger's cup. Waiting.

It wasn't unlike her to leave an email unanswered for days, a week or longer. We both lived our lives on the road. We had a standing agreement to keep communications to a minimum when one or both of us was on tour. I had learnt, however, to read the tone of her silences. This one had a certain ring.

Elke. What to even call her? This was always a bone of contention. My girlfriend? Partner? Collaborator? Lover? All and none of these things? I don't fucking know. Elke who remained ever resistant to labelling our relationship as anything in particular.

This was an ideological matter, she told me. *No person is anyone's anything.*

Yes, sure, I said, *but practically speaking, what do I call you?*

And she said: *Call me Elke. That's my name, isn't it?*

Fair enough, I thought.

We had first met in a warehouse in Rotterdam, both of us rolling on strong Dutch pills. The promoter introduced us. It was a pretty standard-issue techno party, but they had booked a few ambient acts to warm the room up before the DJs arrived. I was by no means at the top of the bill, but I remember enjoying my set that night. Feeling settled in my flow. There were maybe fifty people in the room when I played, most of them just lurking and waiting for the party to start. When we were introduced, Elke helped herself to one of my cigarettes and said she'd missed my set. That was a lie, she told me much later. *I lied because at the time, I didn't know what to make of your music. I didn't know if I liked it or not. But I knew I wanted to fuck you.*

We did fuck, that night, messily on a bench in a dark corner of the party. It was the sort of muffled excuse for sex that happens when you're way too high, all numbness and groping and stifled intensities. But: the music was good.

I remember that night, saying something like: *Do you get that tidal feeling? The bump and the swell? What I get from music now is what the ocean gave me, once.*

She shrugged and said she wasn't much of a swimmer. Our bodies, chemically porous, joined in sychronous motion to a swallowing pulse. Our bodies which collided strangely from the start. Strange enough to produce a compelling dissonance. Strange enough to do it again.

Call me by my name. Not by what I am to you. Call me whatever.

Elke was my whatever at three months, and remained my whatever at four years. Those four years, the four years I spent loving a woman I shouldn't have: we spent those four years for the most part travelling the roads between various central European cities, making and playing music together, mutually convinced this luminosity could keep us warm. It did, up to a point.

In the course of four years, I lost track of how many times I had found hairs on her pillow that weren't mine. We were never monogamous, we had our agreements. But in practice they mostly applied to her. I lost track of how many jealous rages she flew into over such and such a person she imagined was flirting with me in front of her. I lost track of how many bottles she'd thrown at me, and I lost track of her apologies. I lost track of how many times she stormed out and slammed the door, and of how many times I opened it again, when she knocked. I lost track of a lot of things. So it goes.

So it goes. She had those words, lifted from *Slaughterhouse-Five*, inscribed in cursive on the inside of her left thigh. But, when Kurt Vonnegut wrote those words, he was writing about a war, wasn't he?

I'm still not sure exactly what those words meant to her, or why she felt the need to place them somewhere so tender. I'm not sure what kind of war it was she thought she was fighting, but for a while at least she was fighting it with me. We called it love. Maybe it was both. I don't think either of us were equipped to tell the difference.

Lulu is scrawny. Her bones shift underneath a thinning slick of grey fur. She moves slowly and silently, with the kind of sangfroid that is the way of old cats. She has a spot on the windowsill in the sunroom: from there she can keep a watchful eye on the avian traffic. The currawongs are generally too cautious to come that close to the house, but we can count on daily visitations from birds of more brazen nature. Magpies, mostly. The azalea just beyond the balustrade belongs to a chirruping multitude of lorikeets. The balustrade itself has been claimed by a kookaburra. Solitary, as kookaburras always are; tweedy and smug as an old man's slipper.

Lulu has a thing for that kookaburra. She really hates him. She'll sit there serenely for hours until he shows up, then she starts up with her shuddering cat-barks.

Lulu was there on the sill, yowling at this most despised bird, when I sat myself down on the blue sofa to check my emails. Elke's name appeared, in bold. My breath caught in my throat. A dark bloom in my chest.

She started her email with professions of great love and respect. It was with sadness that she was informing me that she would not be joining me here as planned. She would, instead, be going on tour with her flatmate. A harmless sort of person, one of seven people who shared her house, with whom I had eaten a few meals but had no particularly strong feelings about. Just another German punk dude in his thirties, a guy with two pairs of pants, a room full of guitar amps, rich parents and no bedframe. An ineffectual sort whom, she informed me, she had been fucking without my knowledge for about three months, and with whom she was now deeply and irretrievably in love.

I remember witnessing my hands, their mechanical motion, as they slowly and smoothly closed the laptop. I remember the roaring silence, the rising of my blood.

I looked up. Lulu had pivoted her head to face me. The black ridge of her lower lip was slightly ajar. She held my gaze in hers for what felt like a long time, before dropping silently off the bench. She moved over to me and jumped up onto the sofa. Placed herself purposefully, the line of her spine pressed to my thigh.

I was aware of a soft breeze on my feet. I was aware of the ticking of the clock in the hallway. I was aware of Lulu's breathing, the gentle pulse of her little body. Shallow breaths gave way to longer ones. And slowly, into a low, rhythmic purr.

The quiet. The hours. The birds. I listen to the birds. Listening is a cure for noise.

If you leave the window open, this room is perfectly aspected to receive the morning and evening chorus of birds and other creatures. Painters or photographers are known to prize these transitory periods in the day for the singular quality of the light. The same can be said for their sonic character. There are many ways to understand time's passage that don't involve discrete divisions into the units we call seconds, minutes, hours, days. The organic logic of time – the rhythm of birdcall and tidal rivers – is a language worth learning. Especially when time is something you suddenly have a lot of, and you find it moving slowly.

At daybreak, you'll hear the first rumbles of the oyster boats and, shortly following that, the clear first calls of the birds.

Kookaburra and currawong rule this time.

By midday the tinny churning of the oyster boats has ceased and given way to the deeper rumbles of pleasure craft, which last out the afternoon.

Magpie and butcherbird rule this time.

Crow rules the late afternoon, its descending call. The last boat can be heard trundling off into the distance towards the marina, and the traffic on the bridge settles.

Night sounds rise: first, the squabbling of flying foxes as

they settle to feed in the fig trees. Then, finally, the magnificent, penetrating thrum of cicadas and frogs.

The darkest hours of the night belong to the koels. They start to sing in the hour or so before sunrise. Occasionally – very occasionally – you'll hear a koel's call in the daylight hours, but only ever preceding a rainstorm.

The regularity of this succession is one thing I can cling to, in the chain of hours.

This room: the window, the single bed in the corner. The agapanthus, the solid wooden desk, laid out with what I have of my gear. A tangle of black boxes and patch cables.

My full studio set-up would usually include: an Arturia MiniBrute analog synth, Korg SQ-1, Roland SP-404, BOSS RC-30, Eventide TimeFactor, Yamaha DDS-20M, BOSS digital delay-3, BOSS MT-2, Devi Ever LP Overdrive, a zoom recorder, an audio interface, and a TASCAM MF-P01 four-track cassette recorder.

That constitutes about twenty-two kilograms of gear. Transporting the flycase was Elke's job, the cargo booked on her ticket. So I'm marooned now without most of my kit. I'm stuck with the few bits that I brought in my carry-on. I'm back to what would have probably been my first-ever set-up: the Arturia synth with its duo-octave keyboard (easily my most beloved – and expensive – piece of equipment, which I wisely decided not to leave in her care); a chain of three effects pedals and a delay, patched one into the next to make a feedback loop; and an interface which connects all of that to the line-in on my laptop. My zoom recorder, an external mic and a bunch of memory cards. My desktop is cluttered with files and half-finished tracks, all the things that she and I were working on before I left.

Her new lover plays in a shitty vegan straight-edge hardcore band. I guess she plays in a shitty vegan straight-edge hardcore band now, too. I'm sure she's having shitty vegan straight-edge hardcore sex right this minute.

What I have is: time. I have this house full of elegant, mostly empty rooms. A desk with a garden view. I have a bed with room for my body alone, and the company of a moody cat.

I also have: three pedals, a little synth, a zoom recorder and two hundred and twenty-five .wav files worth of field recordings. Taken mostly from the northern Italian and Austrian alps and the forests of southern Germany, the shipyards of Hamburg, and the industrial zones of countless unnamed middle-European towns. The songs of mountains, the ghost hymns of European industry.

We had collected many of these together, mostly during the course of a three-day drive south from Berlin to Zagreb. There I had been contracted by a dance company to score a show that was in development, the kind of bread-and-butter contract that would have paid my rent for three months. The daylight hours I spent in rehearsal with a domineering French choreographer, composing the accompaniment to his work. At night Elke and I would stay up late and work together on our own material. We were working on an album, our first and only collaborative LP. We were using field recordings and analog feedback, cutting live audio from a chain of pedals with found samples collected on the road. The single, rickety Ikea table of our serviced apartment was a snare of cables and controllers. We worked there and ate our meals on the floor; my pay cheque was enough to keep us both comfortably in beer and börek for the time we were there.

That was a special time. I won't say it's easy, trying to finish a thing you half made with the person you loved, who just cast you adrift. Who is carrying on without you in another hemisphere. I won't say it doesn't burn.

I will say: one day, not long after we met, she looked at me and said: *You're a better musician than me.*

At the time, I mistakenly took that as a compliment. I realise, now more than ever, that she didn't mean it that way.

I show up. I listen. I wait. I have the windows closed and my headphones on. This commitment keeps me afloat. Holds back the swallowing tide. I show up. I listen. I wait. I haven't been able to eat. A cup of black coffee has gone cold in front of me, lurking scum clouding its surface.

The atmosphere seethes with unheard songs. A vibrating object produces waves, which alter the pressure of the surrounding air. These waves, or oscillations, are picked up and interpreted by mammalian auditory processing organs as sound. All matter is vibration. All vibration produces sound. But the audible range for human ears is so narrow compared to other species. And the whole schema by which we measure sound is based on the capacities of the human ear. Sonic perception can be quantified using a number of metrics, but the most common are hertz (frequency) and decibels (volume). In decibels, we start at zero, the lowest limit of our audible range. 15 dB is a whisper. 140 dB is a gunshot. 235 dB is a military sonar.

Humans, like other living creatures, are more palpably affected by all the things we can't hear than the things we can. Very low frequency infrasound, anything between 6 and 16 Hz, is outside of audible range but has been found to produce unnerving perceptual disturbances in laboratory tests on human subjects. This frequency, the so-called Ghost Frequency, produces apparitions. Test subjects exposed to infrasound have reported vivid experiences of spectral presences. Cadavers have been used to test the potential of infrasound as a sonic weapon: a low enough frequency, within a certain decibel range, has the power to shatter a skull and degrade tissue. Silence can also be weaponised: most people can only withstand a few minutes of complete silence, the kind of deep-space silence that can only be achieved in an anechoic chamber. There's not really any such thing as silence; there are just things we can hear, and things we can't.

There are ways to give audible form to sub-audible phenomena: the sound of energy itself, the waves and currents that are the real substance of the universe. Analog machine instruments do this, or at least that's how it feels to me. That's the thrill of it. I was eighteen the first time someone showed me how to patch three guitar pedals together to make a feedback loop. Probably the same three pedals I have on the desk in front of me today.

At that time, I was lurking around the edges of the local punk

and metal scenes. I was surrounded for the most part by Boys
Who Play Guitars. I didn't play guitar. At that point, I didn't play
anything.

I was hanging out at a girl's house. A girl I had a crush on,
obviously. She had an original Throbbing Gristle T-shirt, shredded
at both sides to reveal that wedge of skin between her waist and
her black mesh bra. She made it her business to show me a thing or
two. She was in a few bands, and worked days at Allans Music, and
used her staff discount to amass a large collection of effects pedals.
That afternoon, when I was over at her house, she was unboxing a
new one. She said: *I been fucking around with these a bit.*

She patched a chain of three pedals directly to an amp and
turned them on. I remember watching her fingers twisting the
dials on each of the pedals, making micro adjustments to the
frequencies that produced swoops and booms and mutterings, the
sound of energy folding back on itself, summoned forth from the
void of oscillating currents.

I remember her finding a low, rich drone and coming to rest
there. Both of us lying on the carpet next to the amp. I felt like
I was liquefying. In my teenage soul I felt like I had started a
conversation with Chaos herself, and that was an ecstatic discovery.

Everything I have done since has been an extension of that
moment. Every time I show up to work, I'm still an eighteen-
year-old playing with pedals. I have to be. Firstly: you can't do
what I do for a living and pretend you're an adult – the absurdity
of it will overwhelm you. Secondly: every time I show up to work,
I have to arrive with the same eagerness to lean into the static.
Or worse: into silence. Listening is a cure for noise.

~

That said: there are days. There are empty, frustrating days, and today is one of them. I've been sitting here for hours, trying to milk something interesting out of these three little boxes, getting nowhere.

I mute the playback and pull my headphones off. My ears ring.

I cradle my forehead in my hands and press my ears firmly closed with my thumbs.

I hear, first: the muffled sounds of the room. The creaking chair, the scraping of the balls of my feet as I shift them underneath me, the distant sound of a barking crow.

Then: the pop and squelch of spinal fluid and knuckles unclenching.

Slowly, slowly, getting louder: a low, low, low pulse. Low, low, low, *low*, *low*. Thud. Thud. Thud.

I sit like this for a long time. Let my attention become absorbed in the sound of my heartbeat and my steady breath. Audible proof that I am still here, and that my body is my own.

Every second day, I make the long walk down the hill for supplies. There is only one way into town, and that's the same way I came: right on to Caulfield Road, then all the way down. Past number 86. The permanent residence of Marta Baird, the occasional residence of her stoner brother Ross, and formerly her children, my cousins, though they are long gone now.

Marta knows I'm here. We talked about my visit before I flew out. I still know her landline number by heart, because it hasn't changed in twenty-five years. I called from Berlin to let her know my plans. I heard her voice. The warmth of that voice in a hard winter. She was never one for big phone chats, but a few words were enough. She just said: *You know the drill, bub. Door will be open.* Because it always was. Door will be open.

The house is guarded from the street by a thicket of conifers and she-oaks. Through the shady spray of their branches, I can see the exterior walls; crumbled arcs of grey stucco, desiccated vines. The brown door has the number 86 written in chalk.

It was a fancy house in its day, I guess. Spanish mission style, built around the same time as the big places on the hill. A house born of circumstance, which went on to live a different sort of life. At one time it was the biggest and best-looking house on Caulfield Road. It was flanked on all sides by fibro surfer shacks in Fruit Tingle tones, surfboards and sea kayaks stacked against their outside walls, sarongs for curtains. They're mostly gone now, those old houses, along with their original occupants. Replaced by low-maintenance villas and chic bungalows for seasonal rental.

Over the years, the house was home to a shifting cast of humans and animals. I was one of them, I guess. Marta and my mother were sisters. Not by blood. But that's how they loved each other. So this is where I always came for different amounts of time – sometimes for weeks, or months; on one occasion for more than a year – for different reasons. That house, which hasn't changed. Door will be open.

I sit on the neighbour's fence, watching. The windows are dark, there are no cars in the drive, everyone is out. I sit for a long time. It's hot and still. Nothing moves. No cars, no breeze. No human voices. Suddenly, out of the corner of my eye, a dark blur of movement. A currawong swoops and alights on the edge of the roof. Turns its black throat to the sky.

I wander past the school, past the place where the bloodwood tree once stood, and finally into town. Past the bakery, which sells the same lurid pink finger buns (Marta's favourite: the plain ones with the white coconut frosting; raisins made her grimace – squashed flies, she called them) and sweaty cheese and bacon scrolls as I remember, as well as proud rows of tiger loaves with the cracked orange crust. 'Special Bread', as it was known in the Baird residence, the kind only ever purchased for picnics or parties. Past the newsagent and, following that, the remains of what was the Video Ezy, now vacant. Pale blue carpet tiles scattered with broken plaster.

After that comes the entrance to a small covered arcade leading to the supermarket car park. The arcade was derelict for a long time, most of the shops shuttered except for the coin laundry. The area was designated territory for the local high school seniors, and any detour through there would involve kicking through a groundcover of empty chip packets, fag butts, nang canisters and other adolescent debris.

That's changed, though. It's been bought up and redeveloped, fairly recently I would say. It's now home to a bulk health-foods supplier and a series of shops that seem to sell nothing but fancy knitwear and scented candles. I wonder how these shops survive when there's still no-one around to buy their shit.

On the other side of the mall there is a little supermarket, which remains comfortingly dingy, and Hartfield's, a pharmacy-cum-ice-creamery, where a single scoop of hokey-pokey set you back about seventy cents in 1993. Marta, Jack, Ngaire and I had a special ritual for the occasional days when Marta wasn't on shift in the afternoon: she would take us to Hartfield's for a scoop of hokey-pokey, then walk us down to the ferry wharf to talk to the pelicans.

I buy myself a cone after finishing my grocery shopping. The price has gone up to four dollars, but the flavour hasn't changed. I take my prize, coiled in a paper napkin, and make my way slowly down to the water.

It's quiet. The last ferry left hours ago. The jetty looks small and lonely. Low tide. Bilge-funk rising. A fringe of dark kelp skirts the water's edge.

I'm sucking the milky drizzle out of the base of my cone and watching the pelicans glide through the water. I look around. The beach is empty. The sun is starting to go down. I can feel a night-drop coming, a slight chill biting into the air.

I suddenly become aware of two figures to my right, a little further down the sand. So still I had failed to notice them before: two elderly women. They are thin, tall and very upright. They're motionless, feet planted, arms linked, facing the water. The wind gently shifts their hair, which is identically slate grey and bobbed at the nape.

I finish my ice cream and crumple the napkin in my hand. I watch them for a long time. Wait for them to move. But they are perfectly still, except for the motion of the wind in their grey hair.

I'm startled by the sudden, too-close screech of a gull. The bird alights at my feet and starts loudly savaging the remains of a pizza crust. It pulls my gaze away from the women for a moment.

By the time I look back at them, they've turned around. I see their faces. They share the same wide-set jawline. The one on the left is drawing on a cigarillo. They are not made-up or adorned in any way, though they are sharply dressed, despite the sweltering heat: cream shirts, crisply ironed. One in tailored trousers, the other in a box-pleated skirt of deep blue. Sturdy, polished, laced-up shoes.

They move slowly over the sand. The one on the left – the smoking one – walks purposefully forward with a sharp eye. Her companion, supported and contained by the gentle crook of an arm, shuffles beside her, a little tentative, her eyes searching the distance.

The one on the right cranes her neck in my direction. Her gaze settles on me, and darkens. Her jaw goes slack. She plants her feet, pulling her companion to a halt. She looks right at me as though she knows me. I stare back at her. There is something vaguely familiar about her face. Though from this far away and in the dying light, she could be anyone.

The other woman looks up at me, exhales. Turns back to her friend, before gently urging her along.

From my desk, I gaze out over the terrace. The bobbing heads of the agapanthus.

At irregular intervals, Lulu enters, makes a single slinky figure eight around my ankles and departs again.

After some hours at the desk I find myself submerged. After hours and hours of staring out the same window, and working over and over and over the same four-minute section of audio, I need a breather.

I pick up my zoom recorder, a mic and my headphones and take it all with me. It's coming up to sunset, which means I might catch some nice textures in the garden.

I walk over the expanse of grass and around the edge of the property, through the shrubbery, under the scattered shadows of trees. To my right, through a thatch of branches, I can glimpse the waters of the estuary, glowing platinum bright. To my left, the house. All its constituent parts: the terrace; the back door; the dark, unblinking window of my room. Capacious from the inside, but from here, just a house.

When the mosquitoes start to gnaw my ankles I wander back inside. I go to the kitchen and drink a glass of water. Rummage in the fridge, stuff a handful of cold ham in my mouth. I see that Lulu's bowl is empty and shake some biscuits into it. I flick the kettle on in the full knowledge that I do not want a cup of tea and I will not make one. I'm just looking for something else to do and anywhere else to be other than in my room, at the fucking desk.

Eventually, I find myself upstairs again. In the strange suite of rooms adjacent to the master bedroom.

I realise I haven't been up here since that first day I arrived. I take a look around: the green chaise, the armchair, the crystal decanters. The only disturbance is the playing cards; the deck that had been poised on the edge of the table has been knocked off and scattered over the ground. I gather them up and place them back where they were.

These rooms, which had struck me as so elegant when I arrived, now seem squalid and airless. I throw open the windows. The drapes billow.

I lay myself out on the green chaise near the window and a bolt of sunlight cuts across my torso and thighs. It's been a hot day.

Ahead of me, I can see through the open French doors into that other room. That empty room with its big windows. Lulu is reclining on the rug, facing the window, tap-tap-tapping her tail.

There are hundreds of samples and field recordings on my zoom, identifiable only by dates and timestamps. I decide it might be a good time to listen through them and clear the debris from the memory card.

I put my headphones in and listen to the first cluster. The first six or so recordings are all train-carriage ambience. I make a habit of recording trains. I don't often use these samples in music; I just like to collect them. No two trains sound exactly alike. Underground trains, in particular, have their own songs to sing, and the pitch and timbre is unique from place to place, city to city: the Tokyo underground has a soft, droney buzz, like a beehive; the London tube wails; the New York City subway is the most steadily rhythmic but also the wheeziest.

I listen through these ones and I can't tell exactly where they were recorded but, based on the clipped German voice announcing a station name I don't recognise, I am guessing it's Cologne or Munich. Either way, it was not a memorable train, nor are the recordings particularly interesting. I delete them all except one.

I open another file. It's only a few seconds long. The first thing I hear is the sound of a finger being dragged over a mic and the hollow clunk of a jack being removed. The sound of two voices. Mine and Elke's. I can't make out what we're saying to each other. I hear my own voice, muffled, speaking from the other side of something. I think I hear myself say something like *accidents happen*. With a rising inflection. *Accidents happen?* Then, close to the mic, I hear Elke's breath catch in her throat. It's distinct: that particular, glottal sound she always makes in the second before she laughs. I feel a rush of heat to my face. The recording cuts out.

The next file takes me a moment to identify. At first I thought it might be another train. But its edges are softer and cleaner. Organic.

I listen, and as I do, the day I recorded it vividly comes back to me.

We were on the second day of a drive back to Berlin from somewhere. Padua, I think. We were somewhere on the outskirts of a Bavarian forest, driving through the mountains.

We had spent the previous night freezing in the van on the Austrian border in a town called Heiligenblut. The blood of saints. The name amused us both. (*So metal*, we concurred.) However, that night the temperature was expected to hit minus twenty-three, so we were not aiming to spend that evening in a similar fashion, and were struggling to make it to Nuremberg before dark.

Elke was driving. She was angry about something, gripping the steering wheel and turning too sharply into every bend of the narrow, snow-choked roads. More than once I asked her to slow down and more than once she responded with silence. I looked out the passenger window and down the steep face of the mountain. I remember thinking: it wouldn't be so bad. It would be quick, and then this and everything else would be over. Snow would cover our bodies.

We descended and descended and descended, down and around that mountain, which felt endless, further into the glowering gunmetal of an approaching ice storm. I was silently coming to terms with the fact that we were going to be stuck in the van overnight again, and that the possibility of both of us freezing to death was a real one.

We rounded a bend in the road and, all of a sudden, everything was clear. The snow ceased, and bright sunlight cut through the spruces. The road opened up on both sides into flat wide fields, thickly covered with snow and pristine. All that absolute white against the absolute black of the mountains.

We looked at each other and, without saying anything, decided to stop. We pulled off the road. Elke pushed herself away from the steering wheel, let her head drop backwards, exhaling. I threw open the passenger door and immediately jumped out, my feet sinking two feet deep into the snow.

I realised we were parked in front of a small church. There was a memorial shrine attached, as is often the case in that part of the world. Both looked like they had been closed for a long time.

I walked around the outside of the church and found all the doors were locked. I approached the shrine. The little wooden door yielded. Inside: plastic flowers and rows of burnt-out candle stubs. Rows and rows of framed photographs, the monochrome faces of German soldiers, mirthless under glass.

I heard the crunch of Elke's footsteps approaching. I turned around and saw her dark outline, receding into the trees, wading through the waist-deep snow. Against good sense, I followed her. I remember the incredible stillness, as if the forest were holding its breath. Nothing but the *crunch-crunch-crunch* of footfall in snow. But somewhere ahead I could sense the pull of something. Some movement, some pulse.

Elke never cast a glance behind her. She walked, I followed. Through the trees and finally to the edge of a steep embankment. We climbed down through wild beds of ivy and found ourselves at the edge of a stream.

Just like trains, no two bodies of moving water sound the same. They are as distinct as any other sentient voice. The song of that water was crystalline. Totally and utterly clear. My recorder was in the pocket of my anorak, where I always kept it.

It's a four-minute recording. I lie on the chaise in the sun, with the windows open. I put my headphones in and set the playback to loop.

I can hear everything: I can hear the snow on the ground and the colour of the sky. I can hear the branches of birch trees, fringed with talons of ice. I can hear the smoothness of those rocks and the coldness of the water, and for a second I feel as I felt then. Clean. I allow my attention to relax deep, deep, deeper into it, into every icy curl and whisper.

Time passes. Breath slowed to nothing. My hands are heavy

and open. The sound of the water, the sound of the water, the sound of water. And another, deeper space of listening that opens beneath it.

I wake. It's dark. The cicadas thrum. I don't know how long I've been here or how long I've been sleeping.

In the corner of my eye I see a red light. My zoom recorder is on the floor beside me. The LED display is flashing, telling me the memory is full.

I examine the display closer. My eyes are gummed up and blurred. At first I think I'm mistaken so I rub my eyes and take a second glance. The playback has stopped. The device is recording. I must not have locked it. I'm not sure how but, in the process of sliding off my lap and onto the floor, the record function was initiated.

I look at the display: 4:36:22. I have been lying here, recording the sound of my own sleeping carcass, for four and a half hours.

My nights are deep and soundless. I have stopped dreaming. Clammy, twisted in the sheets. Four am. Some nights, the darkness is soft and generous. Other nights, it turns. Shrinks. Fills with panic. Tonight is one of those.

I've heard it said that we process heartbreak in diminishing oscillations. A möbius flow between acute pain and acute numbness.

I can fill my days. I can work. I can pace around the many rooms of this elegant, empty house, look out its many windows. I can keep the tide at bay. I can tell myself stories – truthful stories – about who she was and what I've been extracted from. I can get some relief from the knowledge that this is the last of Elke's betrayals I will ever have to endure. I can keep the tide at bay.

But at night I find myself in the grip of something murkier. I find myself staying up later and later to avoid what I know is coming the second I slip into this single bed. That's when it hits me. The overness of it. That's something I don't know how to feel.

I don't lie here and think of all the times she was an utter cunt. I don't find myself full of righteous relief that the ordeal of loving her is over. Because it's not. Not even close. In this single bed, alone, at four am, I am just a body feeling keenly into the absence of another body. The horrible space around my waist where her sleeping arm should be.

I remember one breakfast, after a show. I was making us pancakes. That was what I always did after a fight. I stood in the kitchen of whoever's apartment we'd crashed in the night before, making us pancakes while she scrolled on her phone, her socked feet propped up on a chair. Watching the bubbles rise in the raw batter, I levered the spatula underneath, and as I did my wrist panged. We'd been fighting the night before and she'd grabbed it, hard. Her grip had fallen right on the site of an old break. That morning, as the pain shot up my arm, I heard a voice say, clearly: *Those who do it once will do it again.*

I answered back: *Tell me something I don't already fucking know.* Flipped that pancake. Slapped it on a plate.

It was never the violence that undid me. Violence, I can handle. Probably a little too well. What always spooked me about her was not the outbursts, but how quickly things would get back to normal. One minute she'd have me pinned to a wall, in a back alley in some town or other, screaming in my face, the yeasty funk of cheap beer on her breath. The next: pancakes. So it goes.

I sit up. Move to the window. Stare out across the terrace and into the garden, at the bobbing heads of the agapanthus, backlit by moonlight.

I quit smoking a year ago. What a fucking stupid idea that was. I can't remember the last time I was hanging for a dart this bad. This was certainly a smoker's house: there's that acrid undertow to the general smell of the place. Sometimes, I'll be hit by a waft of what smells for all the world like a freshly lit cigarette, which lingers for a second, then vanishes.

There's nothing like the smell of a freshly lit cigarette to topple a reformed smoker's resolve. It was in this town that I smoked my first cigarette. I did a lot of things for the first time here, but that's the one I remember most vividly and with the greatest pleasure. I was behind the toilet block on the dunes with Ngaire, who had stolen a couple from Marta's bag. I think we were about nine or ten. Knowing the flogging that was coming to us if we got busted obviously only added to the thrill. Both our mothers were nurses and pack-a-day champions. Marta smoked Longbeach and Mum, who favoured the fresh kick of menthol, smoked Alpine. *Never start this shit* was the warning, sharply delivered every time the paper lip was torn from a fresh pack. Never start this shit.

~

The weeks and months I spent at Marta's house over the years, I mostly spent sleeping in a special makeshift bedroom, a section of hallway cordoned off by way of an old bookshelf and a tablecloth tacked to the rafters. I slept in Jack's old bed, a single day bed just like this one, with a little window, just like this one, also with a view of a row of agapanthus, just like this one.

The hallway itself was long, running all the way from the lounge, past Marta's bedroom, to the combined bathroom and laundry out the back. The house would mutter and creak to itself at night. Possums would squabble in the roof. Strange scraping sounds and knocks and spectral footfall could be heard in that hallway at odd hours. So many times I remember being woken up by what I thought was the sound of Marta traipsing down the hall, returning from a late shift. I came to recognise the difference between Marta's weighty steps and the others, which were lighter and quicker, as though they belonged to a very small person. They would stop and start. Sometimes I got the sense that someone was peering at me from behind my tablecloth curtain. I would pass tense hours under the quilt, listening. Barely breathing.

The sudden waft of cigarette smoke on the air meant one thing: Marta was home from her shift. The smell of cigarette smoke, and the call of the koels. Marta would be sitting in the kitchen having a smoke and a cuppa in the wee hours before bed, and I wasn't alone anymore.

I am seized by a piercing, singular determination to find cigarettes. I take every awful, stagnant, swampy feeling I've been holding on to for the last five hours in this room, in this fucking bed, and sublimate them into this imperative. *There have gotta be some smokes in this house.* Somewhere.

I get up, throw the hallway light on and start rummaging. I look in all the likely places – desk, bureau, pantry, bottom kitchen drawer. All the places you'd stash an emergency pack. Then it occurs to me that a good spot to look might be the little card table in the upstairs sitting room.

I make my way up the dark stairwell and across the mezzanine. Flick the light and look around. Open the little drawer under the side table: I almost leap with joy for a moment when I turn up a packet of menthol Mores in the drawer of the side table. Groan deeply when I realise it's empty. Slump on the chaise.

I lie there under the bright overhead light. I allow my eyes and thoughts to wander, finding them drawn back, repeatedly, to those open French doors, leading into that other room.

Finally, I get up and walk in there. This room. What even is this room? This room that used to be something that it is no longer.

I walk a weary circle around the edges of the rug. Scuff my feet over it. A cloud of grey cat fluff is loosened from the pile, and insinuates itself between my toes.

The wallpaper is brightly pearlescent in the overhead light. Peachy beige with shadows of darker brown caused by age or smoke or sun, maybe. I look down at my feet, then at the rug and notice, for the first time, four deep divots in the pile. Each roughly the diameter of a soda can, equidistant, squarely placed at the corners. I notice the glass cabinet by the window, stuffed to its ribs with papers, stacks and stacks of cream papers, a tasselled key turned fast in the lock.

I notice the drapes. The heavy drapes, which I was certain I had left open, are closed.

'Champion Ruby, please.'

'Fifty or twenty-five?'

'Fifty. And papers.'

The servo has been fancied up a lot since I last saw it. Or corporatised, more accurately. It's a big, bright, twenty-four-hour Mobil now, where it used to be just two pumps and a red-brick pay station that was only open till nine, seven on the weekends. You could get milk and cigs and motor oil there; and there was a small snack selection: out-of-date Cheezels and heat-speckled chocolate frogs or milk duds, cheap sandy-textured chocolate doled out in plastic baggies. Now the lights are bright and always on, it's air-conditioned, the counter is stocked with at least seven different varieties of KitKat, and the attendant (who is maybe seventeen, brown eyed, lanky) works behind a plane of plexiglass. I pour myself a watery-looking coffee from the machine and pay for that along with my tobacco.

I decide I will hold off rolling that first, fast-breaking cig for myself until I get to the beach, because I want it to be perfect. I sip my coffee and wander the main street, past the shuttered shopfronts. I follow the smell of the bakery – the cloying warmth of all that white bread. Theirs is the only light on, pooling on the pavement.

I get to the end of the shops, past the bowlo, and find the stump where the bloodwood used to be. It's been cut right low to the roots, some time ago it would seem: the wood is grey, the grain is smooth, almost felty to the touch. One of the many men I called Uncle when I was a kid (though this one, I'm sure, was an actual relative, one of Mum's much older brothers) just called it Medicine Tree. He had forgotten its proper name. He told me that we use the leaves to smoke ourselves clean, that we use the sanguine resin to treat toothache.

I used to pass this tree every day on my way home from school, and would often stop to break off some of the garnet-red pitch in the absent-minded, entitled fashion of a child. I would take home fistfuls of the stuff, balance the lumps on the notches of my fingers like jewels. Imagining myself adorned, beautiful.

About twenty metres past the stump is the gate to the primary school. Kinder to grade six only, probably no more than a couple of hundred students in total when I went there.

Hurricane fencing at chest height. There used to be a gap in the fence right at the back-left perimeter, concealed by bottlebrush scrub, immediately behind the toilet block. If you were gonna wag that's how you'd exit without being seen. I remember the day that I, a humble grade four kid, was shown where the hole was by a grade six kid, and was aware at the time that I had come into a hallowed piece of knowledge.

Breaking into the school after dark was regular sport for all the older kids, especially the grade sevens, who by that point had all left for the high school out past the north headland. There were always security cameras mounted on the corners of the buildings but half of them were busted, and if you stuck to the perimeter, just inched your way around the fence through the scrub, you could evade their scope.

The fence doesn't look like it's been fixed in twenty years. In fact, the school is maybe one of the very few buildings in the whole town that hasn't had a makeover. The town might have grown in some ways, money-ways mostly, but it's an ageing population. Other than those boys on the jetty that morning I arrived, I don't think I've seen many kids at all. Not on the beach, not in the street, not anywhere.

The hole is still there. Right where I remember it. I pull back the lip of pliant knitted wire and slip through. My feet find knotted roots; bottlebrush leaves needle my cheeks. I inch my way along a ridge of treated-pine fencing, balancing, placing my feet deliberately. From this vantage point, the school doesn't appear to have changed much. Still the same cluster of ten or so demountables on a patch of baked earth. Sallow beige walls, louvred windows, slack-jawed guttering stuffed with eucalyptus mulch.

The spaces between the buildings reveal themselves: between the library and the tuckshop I can see the quad, the square of bitumen at the centre, where we'd all eat lunch. Those low steel benches arranged around the edges, each catching a temporary sliver of shade with the rotation of the sun. The one on the left-hand side got the most shade during the course of the day and that was where I remember sitting the most with my lunch, which was usually a little bag of cold cocktail franks and sauce, maybe a chip sandwich. An overripe banana that would stink my whole bag out with fruit-funk.

The ground drops away steeply after the blond-brick building that houses, on the upper level, the principal's office and the staff rooms. It's the only building on the grounds, besides the toilet block, that is constructed out of anything permanent. The slope, which leads down to the smallish patch of piebald grass that passes for an oval, reveals the basement level of the building, which houses the music rooms.

I sit on one of the benches – too low, made for primary-school-sized people – and look at the building. Look at the exterior wall of that basement level, specifically. There's a long, thin, high-set row of windows. Too high to see inside or out of.

Between the ages of six and fourteen, I probably spent as much time in basement rooms like that one as I did in any of the places that I called home. Everything in my life was a variable, except piano. No matter where I was, and no matter how many different ways the shit was hitting the fan, for those eight years I sat through two lessons a week and at least an hour of daily practice, up to four hours in my later years, especially if I was preparing for an exam or a recital.

Piano wasn't my choice: it wasn't my choice to be inside practising scales when all the other kids were outside playing football or surfing. But I started so young, too young for questions or refusals. Considering how often we moved, I don't know why my mum couldn't have chosen a more mobile instrument, but she made a lot of impractical choices.

Marta's house had a piano, so during the on-and-off times I lived there I would practise at home. But when I was with Mum I clocked my practice hours at school, after all the other kids had gone home, in rooms just like that one. I remember all those rooms – the sameness of them – in more detail than any of the many spaces where I slept or ate. I remember the damp carpet. I remember the constancy of the temperature. No matter how intense the summer heat was you always needed a jumper, because school music rooms, for some reason, are always cold. I remember how my knuckles and my wrists used to ache.

I went through a string of teachers, at a string of different schools, including this one. I remember Mrs Martin, with the bobbed hair and the gold crown on her right incisor. I remember Mr Howard with his fucking rank breath. I remember Emily, a younger one, who always wore this green fluffy pullover and very high-wedged sandals, which she claimed could ease the strain on a pianist's ankles and calves.

I remember, from this school specifically, another woman whose name I have lost. She must have been one of my earliest teachers, the first even. She was older and spoke with a thick accent. I remember her from the first year spent living with Marta, when I was very young. I don't remember her face, but I remember the rustle of her voice. A smell to her that was elderly and powdery soft but had a certain gravitas. I remember her bony hands extending from starched cuffs, and a ring of heavy, prehistoric amber that sat proud on her left middle finger, a mosquito clenched in its resin eye. She told me: *This stone is older than dinosaurs*, which blew my tiny mind.

The sun is coming up. I watch the pale bricks of that exterior wall warm up slowly as the light rises. Reach into my pocket for my tobacco and roll two cigarettes. One behind my ear and the other in my mouth. Light it.

When I was walking down the hill I could hear the koels. Their song alone, ringing through the dark bush. Crouching in the old schoolyard, sat on that low metal bench drawing on my cigarette, I become aware of their absence. The lights are turning up from underneath: the deep teal of the pre-dawn breaking into brightening shades; paler, paler, paler shades of turquoise; warmer, warmer, warmer into saffron, peach and gold. Silence, for a long time. Until, finally: a riotous kookaburra. The bringer of daylight.

As I leave the schoolyard I stoop to take a sip from the bubblers. A metallic flash of cold water in my throat. I slip out through the fence and follow it back around to the main street. Follow it down. The bakery and the fruit shop and the newsagents are all rolling up their shutters, crates of milk and apples and bound slabs of papers stacked at their doorsteps.

I follow the road around, past the bus stop and the ferry wharf. The tide is high but calm. I keep following the road all the way up the steep incline and over the north headland, down through the saltbush and the dunes of the main beach.

The ocean, dawn-splendid and wild. There are six benches out the front of the surf lifesaving club, all of them bearing memorial plaques for locals lost to the sea. The dates on each one indicate premature deaths, people in their teens, twenties, thirties – surfers drowned in big swell, teen suicides off the south headland. I take a seat on a bench that is named for one: *Andy Fallon, 1988–2009.* I try for a moment to think if I ever knew an Andy Fallon; pull my second cigarette from behind my ear and light it.

There's half-a-dozen surfers out on the break, two others sat on the steps in front of the surf club, their wetsuits peeled half-off. Everything aglow: their skin, the sand, the concrete, the water, their faces; the sand stretching out forever, still cool underfoot at this hour but blazing alight with that distinctly red tinge it has on this part of the coast, a colour I have never seen anywhere but here.

The surfers are always here this early, but it'll be another few hours before the regular traffic arrives, so the beach is otherwise empty. Except – I notice – for one little clump of human belongings resting on the sand about halfway down. I hadn't seen any swimmers in the water when I arrived.

When I turn my head I notice a figure, backlit, rising from the water and walking slowly onto the sand. They move closer and I make out the distinct curvatures of their form, the dense mantle of water-weighted black curls on their shoulders and, eventually, their smile. Her smile. Breaking as white and strong and joyful as a wave.

I should have guessed that Marta would be there at that time. She hasn't missed a morning swim in twenty years.

Marta Baird, a staunch six-foot-two in bare sandy feet at her kitchen table, spooning Nescafé into two chipped mugs. The red mug, the one with the missing handle, and the faded All Blacks mug with the silver fern graphic on it. I remember when that one came home with Marta after a trip home to Aotearoa. Marta hated rugby but she loved that mug, because it had been a gift, and it was big, oversized, for when you wanted a real cuppa. The tablecloth, also a gift – some kitsch bastardisation of Clan Baird tartan, faded thistle green and violet, which has dressed Marta's kitchen table since before I existed. The ring-stains of thousands of coffee cups mapped on its surface like the transits of erratic planets.

Marta: every assured, muscled square inch of her in a loose cotton blouse. The one with the red flowers on turquoise. A torus of greenstone on a leather thong sits at the base of her throat as it always has done. Grey-streaked black curls spill to her waist, still damp, as they have always been. In all my memories of Marta, all the ways I might picture her in my mind, her hair is always seawater-damp.

'Where you been hiding then?' she asks me now.

I don't have much of an answer for her except to say, 'I've been in a bad way. I split up with Elke. It was unexpected.' I hear myself saying more than once that it was unexpected, as if by repeating it I could make it true.

'Elke?' she asks. 'Which one was this one again?'

I remind her, the musician, the one I play music with. She was going to come out here on this visit.

'We were together for four years,' I tell her. 'You were going to meet her. Four years, done.'

She nods and asks, 'You want toast?'

The kitchen is at the front of the house and the table sits in a corner surrounded by open windows. The cicadas are cranking up as the heat rises. We came in the same way we always do, through the always-open front door. A heavy thing that needs a firm push to open. The floors of the old house are in an even greater state of decay than when I was last here; they buckle and shudder under every footstep, the windowpanes shake in their frames. The smell is unchanged. The photos on the walls, the busted old pool table in the front room, the same lawn furniture out the back, half-sunk into the lawn. The piano, where it's always been, in the passageway just past the kitchen door.

'It's just me here now,' Marta says. 'Just little me, in Annie's old room.'

Annie was Marta's broad-chested, Glaswegian mother, though no-one ever called her Mum or Grandma or Aunty, always Annie.

'The ceiling in my room is leaking something chronic. We had a few big storms, kept waking up with water pissing on my face.' She laughs. Her lips peel back to reveal the bluish mercury shadows in her teeth.

The sight of the back garden: the big table, the rusted old tub that was filled with ice and booze for parties, the multicoloured festoon lights that were hung for New Year's some time a decade ago and never came down, the old washing-machine drum that served as a fire pit. This house was always a gathering place, a magnet for people.

Annie threw parties that went for days; tides of people came and drank and left and came again. Well into her eighties she did this. Parties would happen for any reason, at any time. Celebrations for New Year's, or Hogmanay as she called it, involved two days of heavy-duty ritualised house cleaning, followed by a two-day piss-up.

The one and only year this did not happen was the last year of her life, when she was too full of cancer and morphine to host as she would have done. That year, we still gathered, but quietly. I remember Annie's face, reflecting the light of the fire, and I remember Marta singing, as she always did. In the first few sweltering days of January, Annie faded and passed. Peacefully, in the room where Marta now sleeps.

The first pair of feet to cross the threshold of a dwelling in the New Year should always be those of a dark-haired man. That was always how Annie began the yarn of Mike's entrance into her life, as a twenty-one-year-old migrant to this strange colony. That was how they met: at a New Year's party in Sydney. Annie did not recall whose party it was or why she was there, only that a handsome Māori man was the first body to pass through the door of the house after midnight, that he brought whisky. *Good whisky,* she was always careful to add, in her frequent retelling of this story. *It was good whisky.*

Mike was not his real name. His name was Mikaere. That was more than what most Anglo-Aussies could cope with, so he shrunk his name into a single, white syllable. I never met him. I met his brothers and his cousins but I never met Marta's dad; he died when she was a teenager. I got to know his face intimately: his picture sat on top of the piano, next to the turquoise urn that housed Annie in her post-corporeal form. The picture would have been taken not long before he died. A man in his mid forties, leather jacket, smiling on a windy bluff. Marta and her brother, Ross, both resemble him more than their mother. Marta, in particular.

They are still where I last saw them, both of them, on top of that old upright piano, an ancient, toothless thing, moisture-warped and untuned since the 1980s, probably. They are both still there. The piano is still there, in the same place between the door to the kitchen and the door that led into the mysterious cavern that was Ross's flat, one of many ad-hoc additions to the house.

I ask Marta where Ross is.

She shrugs. 'Down south somewhere, I think? Took off for a bit.' She walks ahead of me, past the piano and into the kitchen, in sudden silhouette against the belting late morning sun. 'Just me here now,' she says again. 'Just little me.'

That piano and I have history. It was the first instrument I ever laid my hands on. This was a musical house; everyone who lived here could sing or play. Marta, Annie, the cousins, all the others who came and went. The extended family were all singers and casual multi-instrumentalists, my mother included. Music was just a part of every gathering, a part of every day that passed.

The piano was a major purchase that Annie and her husband had made when they first married. Annie played herself, but she bought the piano for her children, for Marta and Ross. By their own admission, they never showed much interest beyond the fundamentals. Marta could play a few tunes here and there, but mostly she was a guitarist and a singer.

That's how Mum and Marta knew each other to begin with. They were youngsters in the Cross together. Working in bars and playing in bands. I remember driving into Sydney with Mum a handful of times. Sometimes Marta would join us, her and Mum going on a tour of their old stomping grounds.

I saw a different side of both of them when they would get together like that – they'd style up for it. Mum always more femme in her torchy little frocks and Marta a bit edgier in T-shirts and her dead dad's leather jacket, the same one he wore in that photo.

Even though they'd both moved away and had kids and gotten regular-people jobs, they kept in touch with most of their old friends. Those evenings in the Cross would always start with a cruise around in Marta's car. I loved it. Sitting in the back while Mum and Marta talked and smoked and planned the evening ahead – who they were going to see, what gigs they were going to go to, sharing snippets of news about their old crew. They seemed to know everyone. Marta would pull up out the front of the Bourbon and chat to the bouncers; the girls on Forbes and William streets all seemed to know us and so did the boys on the Wall. Sometimes we'd stop by the old Piccolo bar – they'd have coffee, I'd have a Sprite.

Those nights, those women, both of them alive and joyful, nothing like the versions of them that I encountered on the day-to-day. Mum's friend Thursday would babysit me, usually, while Marta and Mum went out. She was a tall woman with a long face and hair like a Lipizzaner stallion, who we would always pick up from the same terrace house on Kellett Street. The sight of Thursday, exiting the building at the end of a shift in slides and an oversized T-shirt, a giant tote bag stuffed with work clothes over one arm, always made me happy. She was funny, and she talked to me like a grown-up, and when we were back at the hotel she'd let me pick the movies we'd watch and sometimes, if she was in a really good mood, she'd let me fuck around with her make-up. I remember how Mum and her always kissed each other lightly on the mouth as they said hello, same as she did with Marta.

Mum was old mates with the concierge at the Sebel, who would always hook us up with the best suites in the house. This was when the Sebel was still a rock-and-roll hotel. I remember once, I guess I was about seven, sitting with Mum and Marta at breakfast one morning and there was this busted-looking dude at the next table with his sunnies on, and a black-and-white shirt with fine polka dots open to the chest, and a generally shadowy air about him, sitting alone and working his way through a massive stack of pancakes.

It was pretty normal to see famous people around the Cross at that time. I thought I already knew famous people, because I'd met Carlotta. But there was something different about this guy. Mum and Marta sipped their coffee silently, both trying to act like butter wouldn't melt, but when the dude finally got up to leave, they both made a lot of heavy, breathy sounds to each other and quaked with stifled giggles. I asked who the man was and they said his name was Bob Dylan.

Those times in the Cross: that's how I want to remember my mother. I want to remember her happy and free and laughing with a bright red mouth. I want to remember her singing. Like Marta, she was a singer. A classical vocalist, a mezzo-soprano in fact. Though during her Cross days I believe she mostly sang in folk bands – it was the 1970s, and she had that Joni Mitchell kind of range.

Mum grew up in care, and singing was one of the things that got her through. In between laundry work there was often singing. Holy music, hymns, but also classical music. Bach cantatas, godly shit like that. She was a good singer. Good enough to audition as a young woman for the Conservatorium, and get in.

She was halfway through her first year when she found out she was pregnant with me, to a man she didn't love and didn't care to raise a child with. That was it for her, or so she decided at the time. She moved, I was born, and we kept on moving. It wasn't her who told me about dropping out of the Con. It was Marta, who was admonishing me for slacking off on practice.

Your mother sacrificed a lot for you, a phrase I heard from Marta's mouth too often. *It's important to her that you have music in your life.*

The only times I heard my mother sing were in this house, in Marta's company. It was as though Marta held the only key to a room that my mother was scared to enter alone.

I know for a fact that Marta has a hard time considering what I make – abstract compositions using found sounds and textures, analog feedback, assemblages of samplings and field recordings, things involving obtuse equipment and special microphones – to be music. Realistically, I don't think of it as music either, which is maybe what means I can keep doing it.

My failed career as concert pianist was precisely what opened the road for my moderately successful career as an experimental composer, and it was in this house, at that piano, that this narrative began. It was Annie who first heard me play. First heard what she described as my 'prodigious' ear for melody.

Mum was having one of her turns, one of her 'tired' times, and she sent me to Marta's for a bit. This would have been one of the first of my extended stints at 86. I guess I was four or so. Nearly five. The afternoon Annie heard me playing is probably one of my earliest memories – gauzy, submerged, but punctuated with weirdly specific details, the way that early childhood memories always are.

Annie loved the classics. She lived in the front room of the house and always had her radio on, always tuned to Classic FM. I was noodling around on the piano one day, and without meaning to played the first few bars of a Grieg concerto I had heard on the radio earlier that day.

Annie was doing the dishes in the kitchen and I remember her rushing in, soapy hands aloft and demanding, in that tar-drawl of hers: *Play that again. Play it back.*

'Does anyone still play that derelict machine?' I ask.

'The piano?' Marta shakes her head. 'Firewood.' She slides a piece of white bread into the toaster and presses the lever, before resting her elbows on the bench. 'Do you still play at all?'

The same question she's asked me every time I've seen her for the last twenty years, and for twenty years the answer has been the same.

We sit in the kitchen and catch up on all the family business. Jack had a baby, still living at Kingscliff, still surfing, very much in love with a girl named Claire. Ngaire is up north, still single, still tending to plants; her vocation from a young age. Ngaire had started growing dope in her teens; by the time she was a high school senior she had a small crop with a steady enough yield to save up to buy herself a little car. The same little car that she drove to Lismore, where she's been ever since, working on farms while she got her degree in horticulture.

Marta shows me a picture on her phone of Ngaire, sanguine and brawny, holding a giant bird of paradise flower in two hands.

The stem is as thick as a broom handle and reaches almost to her feet; she's holding it up like a prize catch.

'Will you look at the fucken size of this thing? The plant itself is as big as a banana palm, apparently,' Marta says. 'I've only ever seen the small ones.' She gestures to a row of them, planted underneath the kitchen window, their flowerheads poking just above the sill. 'She put these in before she left. She said to me, "Mum, even you can't kill these bastards."' Marta laughs. 'Didn't get her green thumb from me, that's for sure.'

I talk about the garden up at the house on the hill. The agapanthus flowers outside my window, how they remind me of this house.

'The agapanthus, oh yeah.' Marta laughs again. 'Those purple things? They are long gone. Bugs got into them. Mum put them in – I never liked them much anyway. Bloody mozzie traps.'

She asks me, 'Which house is it you're staying in again? Up on Terrania Crescent? What number?'

I tell her. 'It's a big place, creamy-coloured, behind a high fence.'

'That describes most of the places up there. Whose place? Do you know who lives there?'

'No-one, right now, as far as I can tell. Maybe a deceased estate? It's half packed up.'

She scrunches up her face and repeats the number; her eyes roll to the left as she searches her memory. 'Doesn't ring a bell.'

Marta crashes out on the sofa around midday, but not before she cuts a couple of Endone from a sheet and puts them into my pocket. 'You've never been a great sleeper,' she says. 'And I know you've had a rough one lately. I don't have any temazzies left but anyway: two of these will knock you out.'

For a really long time, I stay curled on the recliner, listening to Marta snore, her face gone soft and sweet as cake in her sleep. A shrieking gang of cockatoos in the yard do nothing to stir her, nor does the clamour of a surf-rescue chopper flying low overhead.

I leave as quietly as I can over the shaky floor. As I cross the yard, a wind whirrs through the she-oaks, the first breath of an afternoon southerly. The air moving through the spiny foliage of those trees makes a singular and unrecordable sound. I've tried many times to capture it – with different mics, different devices – and always failed. It just comes out sounding like white static. You never get the full dimensionality of it. You never hear the singing of the trees.

By the time I cross the threshold of the house, the sun has dipped below the tops of the trees. Outside: that red hour; that time of deep glow and dying heat. Inside: dim. So quiet.

Ordinarily, upon arriving home, I am saluted at the door by Lulu who, having sensed my approach, sits herself on the hallway table and waits. If my arrival coincides with dinnertime, as it does today, she'll circle my feet and whine emphatically.

I flick on the hallway switch and the one bulb spreads a hazy pool of light. I call out to Lulu. I hear nothing. I move into the kitchen, and call out to her again. Her dish is empty. I reach for her kibble tin, give it a rattle, and call again.

I open the windows. The dry creak of wood. The sound is strangely flat. Every sound is: my footfall on the carpet, the rattle of Lulu's kibble tin, my own voice calling into the dark house. It sounds some kind of wrong. Dampened, as though the walls of the house are absorbing the vibrations that pass between them.

I listen through the open window for the night song of the cicadas, for the frogs and the chattering bats, and hear nothing.

I head to the work room and sit down. Look out the window. The agapanthus, looming at the fringes of the terrace, as usual. My coffee cup, left from my morning session, still sitting on the desk where it was. Everything where I left it. But. Somehow not.

Silence is not a substance. Silence is only the absence of sound, just as darkness is an absence of light. Right now, though, I feel in the presence of silence. As though it were a thing with weight and volume and a looming shape, summoned from negative space.

I pass the evening in an aimless way. I wander the rooms of the house. Smoke. Try to work and fail. Eventually, I flick on the television for company. There is some banal movie, some basic rom-com shit, which I watch while I push sulky, over-boiled ravioli around a plate.

Lulu's dish remains untouched. I listen out for the padding of her feet, for any little thumps or rustles that might herald her arrival. Nothing.

The late news finishes, and I flick off the TV. There's that silence again. I look out through the trees to the moonlit water. I listen into the dark. This darkness, ordinarily so layered with the chattering of nocturnal life. Quiet. Too quiet tonight.

I look at the clock. It's just past ten. I head to my room and lie on my bed in the dark. I'm suddenly aware of the weight of fatigue in my body. Physically, I'm so tired I can barely move. But I can feel my thoughts begin to churn. My shoulders and jaw tensing. Inevitably, my thoughts turn back to Elke. Replays of old dramas (happy ones, ugly ones, all cut together, all mashed up into one horrible master-edit). I want to preserve the good feelings of the day, of my warm morning with Marta. I want to sleep and wake up clean. So I take out the first of the two Endone that Marta gave me, crush it and rail it, saving the second. Then I put some music on.

There are two albums that consistently calm me when I'm frenzied: Cat Power's *The Covers Record* and William Basinski's *Disintegration Loops*. Both albums were released on the turn of the millennium, 2000 and 2002 respectively. They both came into my life around that time. Both came to me as burnt copies through friends. They're portals back into a time when I found myself very much alone, but happily so.

I put Cat Power on first. The languid opening chords of the first track, her iconic cover of 'Satisfaction', reach their tendrils into the dark. I can't hear this song without remembering the first time I heard it. I would have been about eighteen, lying in bed in a terrace house in the city, just before sunrise. I was wearing a stranger's scratchy jumper and coming down off some pretty wretched speed. I remember: the streetlight's glow, the iron lace on the balcony casting florid shadows on the wall, on my outstretched legs.

I love cover versions because, at their best, they are capable of revealing the uncanny inverse of a song you thought you knew. It's the redactions that make this version so distinctly and perfectly its own. She only sings the verses. In doing so, she denies the listener the catharsis of a chorus. It's all simmering build-up, no release. She doesn't need to say she can't get no satisfaction. The tone of her voice makes it clear that satisfaction might not be her goal. The broken space of unsung words that she opens up, between verses, transforms the original – a hymn to whiteboy ennui – into a perfect document of feminine longing. I splay out on the red coverlet in dim light.

I'm reminded of PJ Harvey and Björk's earlier, iconic duet of the same song. Seeing that on TV as a teenager was another moment I remember clearly. Their version embodied something very different, though. Theirs was an explosive mulch of desire and rage. Cat Power's version is the smoke to their fire. She sings quietly through the hollow bones of a forty-year-old song and gives voice to the ache that lives on the underside of things, to all the unnameable, empty feelings that trail extinguished passions.

The Covers Record is a forty-minute album and by the time 'Sea of Love' comes on I'm couched in a comfortable opioid haze and ready to paint on another layer. I crush the second Endone and put on *Disintegration Loops*.

This album is a beautiful accident and a child of decay. When William Basinski unearthed an archive of his old compositions – recorded in the 1980s on analog tape – and attempted to digitise them, he found that the tapes had begun to degrade. Every time the loop passed through the head of the tape deck, a little more of the ferrite flaked off and dissolved, resulting in increasingly layered and ghostly distortions. The album is only two tracks, an hour long in total, the same two short loops on continuous playback, a mesmeric, tidal flow of sonic detritus, expanding and scattering into particles, the apparition of a melody gradually subsumed by static, something ordinary made exquisite by the process of its own organic dissolution.

The happenstance recording that would become this album took place on 11 September 2001. As the legend goes, the composer and his friends listened to the tapes from a shared rooftop in Brooklyn, watching as the Twin Towers came down. I remember that day too, of course I do. I witnessed the World Trade Centre incinerate and collapse from my lounge room in my hometown, oceans away from New York City.

It was not long after my seventeenth birthday, and I had been at school late, practising. I had made it through the heats of the regional eisteddfod and was preparing for an upcoming state competition. It must have been around nine when I got home. Mum and her boyfriend at the time (a hunched, sullen dude called Peter, one in a series of men of a similar genre) were on the couch watching TV. The broadcast was suddenly interrupted by a streaming banner of text at the bottom of the screen. *BREAKING.* I don't remember what the rest said, except that it was vague. Something about a fire. Something about New York. Something about two planes. *BREAKING* punctuated the flow of words; over and over: *BREAKING.* After a minute or so, the screen went to black. I remember that square of black distinctly. That interruption. I remember, too, the sudden appearance of the news anchor, her coral blazer, the glazed confusion on her face, her mouth half open, the long pause of apprehension before she spoke. That silence.

By the time the album finishes I am right on the edge of sleep. But not quite.

My zoom recorder is next to me on the night stand, along with my headphones. I decide to listen to the recording from the Bavarian stream again. I hit play, and let the water run over me.

After a few minutes, the playback falters and cuts out. I check the jack, assuming I must have pulled my headphones out. I haven't. I look at the display, to see if I've paused it by accident, but the LED just shows me my files. Hundreds of them. Distinguishable only by strings of numbers, dates and timestamps.

04.36.22. The most recent recording, the one I made by mistake the other day.

I hit play. What I hear: nothing much, at first. Just atmosphere. Then suddenly swirling up through the bed of whispering frequencies comes the call of a currawong. The astonishing melancholy of that cadence.

I listen to all the sounds of evening descending: the confluence of birdsong, wind, harbour sounds, the wash of noise behind it all. I hear what might be the sound of myself snoring. I hear a breathy shuffle of what might be approaching cat feet and the probing of a curious nose. I hear the hum of boats in the distance.

Minutes tick over. Turn into more minutes. It's a long recording, featuring nothing but birdsong and cicadas and white noise. I let it play. I can hear the afternoon light, I can hear the smell of angophora resin and saltwater, I can hear the redness of the cliffs, I can hear the warmth. I follow the ebbing tide of the drugs towards sleep. Fall into the thrumming pulse of the evening chorus, all my frenzied particles sifting together, plumes of silt in viscous black.

A sudden displacement of air. The size and shape of a body, moving. That sensation. How far away? Next to the bed? By the door? Impossible to tell.

Do I see the hands of the clock in the hall? What do they say? Four? Five?

None of the lights are on, but I can see everything. The colour: I can't describe. Blue? Blueish?

A sudden displacement of air. The size and shape of a body. A beckoning feeling. An urge upwards and towards the door. My feet slide over the floor, cold and too light, as though I'm being pushed along on a cushion of air. Everything is lit from within. The hallway, the kitchen, the sofa, the hallway, the stairwell, the door, another door and another. Suddenly there are new rooms in this house. Appendices and addenda, tiny chambers and hooks in corridors with no purpose, no destination.

The kitchen. The sofa and the television and the phone, Lulu's bowl. The windows, and all the things beyond the windows: the gardens, the inlet, the azalea the agapanthus the angophoras the date palms. None of which is visible to me now. It's just house and more house. Everything where it should be. Everything is here but nothing is the same. Nothing casts a shadow. Everything is in its place but nothing takes up space. It's flat and luminous, like a negative held over a lightbox.

I can hear daylight songs, though here we are beyond night. I can hear the birds.

I can hear daylight songs, moving into evening. I can hear the swooping call of currawong and droning cicadas. I can hear the swell of the evening breeze.

I can hear daylight songs, moving into evening, moving into something else. In between the calls of the birds, in between every other thing, something is pressing gently to be heard. I'm somewhere. Where? Planted at the base of the stairwell. The innermost chamber of a spiral conch. I can hear something – looping on repeat.

My feet find the first step and then the second, and suddenly I'm at the top. I reach the landing, and I cast a glance back. See nothing. The first few stairs, descending into a well of darkness thick as syrup.

The sudden displacement of air.

I know she's here. I know there is someone here.

There's a creeping glow across the wallpaper and the birds, the birds and that sound, that other sound louder, louder now. That sound which is not a sound but a melody. A fragment.

I know she's here.

This room. This room that was a room but has been emptied of itself. The drapes closed. The green rug. So blue – fish-tank blue – in this light, if light is what you call it.

I know she's here. Turn my head to the wall. Turn it back..

She's seated at the piano. The glossy, black expanse of a piano. Her hair is straight and silver, frames her stern jaw. Her hands are spread out on the keys. Her fingers are motionless, but I can hear it. This melody that comes from nowhere but is here, in everything.

It's a tune that I recognise but can't name.

I look down at my own hands. They are not my hands. They are the hands of someone much older than me, fine and very fair but sun-speckled, aged. On my finger is a heavy stone ring. Proudly on the middle finger of my left hand. In it, an ancient glow.

The bones, fanned out under membranous skin and ending in thick knuckles. They are shaking slightly. As I look at them, lines begin to appear, crosshatched in the skin.

They are pale at first, the boiled white of old scars. They grow darker, turning a bruised pink and, finally, the skin begins to split. Before my eyes, deep lacerations open up across the knuckles and wrists. The split tissue glistens, but it doesn't bleed. I watch and wait for blood to come, but the cuts are clean.

I look up again. She has moved away from the piano. She's standing, with her back to me. She moves without moving. One minute she's next to the piano, the next she's flush to the wall. Brings her forehead to touch it and lets her arms go slack. They hang heavy from the shoulder sockets. The melody keeps looping.

For a moment, I am just a body. A set of lungs and a heart that beats easily. For a moment, there is peace. I have made it to another morning. I slept, and now I wake. And that is enough.

But when I open my eyes that feeling drops out from under me. It's pitch dark. The clock tells me it's just after three am. This night is mute.

I am suddenly awake and strung humming-tight. I find myself in the kitchen, lifting a shaky glass of water to my lips.

I look at my hands. Splay them open on the cool marble counter. The skin is smooth and intact but all I can see are those dark, bloodless seams opening across my knuckles. I remember her face; the sight itself is blurred, her features obscured, but I remember it. I don't remember the way she looked, but the way she looked at me.

I walk from the kitchen to the bathroom to the hallway back to the bedroom. Every room I enter feels occupied. The house feels suddenly occupied. I feel suddenly occupied.

A rising anxiety seizes me and I stave off panic by busying myself, attempting to, and failing. Reading is impossible. My eyes dart across pages, scattering syllables, making sense of nothing.

I turn the television on: *Psychic TV* is on, not the band but actual psychic TV, where strangers ring in and a spirit medium in a brightly lit studio answers pointed, desperate questions about their lives. Always the same questions. Almost always about unhappy marriages. A red-headed woman is throwing oracle cards and talking about calling on the Archangel Michael for assistance. She flips a card to face the screen, and I can see him, Michael, sword drawn, linen-draped and astride a bemused Lucifer, the angel pressing his foot into his adversary's muscled chest. The woman holds the image up to the camera for a long time. The blue glare hurts my eyes.

I head into the study, turn on the lamp and open up my computer. Light spills from the window and illuminates the agapanthus. Beyond them, the dark garden.

I find my zoom recorder and remove the SD card, load it into a USB reader and connect. It takes a few minutes for the files to transfer. A series of dates and timestamps appear in the download window: 22.08.2018.03:55.wav 24.08.2018.07:02.wav 03.09.2018.16:32.wav

Finally, the most recent recording appears on the screen. 02.02.2019.18:46.wav. 4 hours, 32 minutes, 22 seconds. I open the file in Ableton. The waveform opens on the screen, powder-blue on grey, flurries of feathery lines and peaks. I hit play.

I hear what I heard the first time: the birds, the birds, the birds, the cicadas, the shifting breeze through a sleeping house.

The longer I listen, the more distinct it becomes: there are two layers to this recording. It has a distinct bi-dimensionality: birdsong, the boats, the sounds from outside; these sounds are happening on one plane. The atmospheric fuzz, this is happening on another. Of course, this is objectively true: both of these sounds are being produced by physically different spaces, inside and outside. But the longer I listen, the more they sound like two isolated recordings that are playing concurrently. There is a sense of space between them, which only grows as I listen.

In one place, I can hear the birds. I can hear life and movement. I can hear some other place, though. This static place. A place with no smells, no heat or light. No passing of time.

I listen deeper. I tune my ears to that other place. The sound of the birds recedes. Deeper still, I begin to hear other things in that cold wash. I hear, for a moment, what I think is a voice, or voices.

Then, distinctly, something I did not expect: I hear seven descending notes.

I hear them again.

There's a pause. And then: again. Seven notes. A fragment of a melody in 2/4 time.

I slam the space bar. Isolate a twenty-second loop. Let it play and replay. Play and replay.

I stop and sit in the dark. The hairs on my arms twitch.

Currawong, clear as a bell.

I don't know how long I lie awake for, and I don't know at what point I fall back to sleep.

My computer is still open, but the music has stopped.

It's eleven in the morning. Stinking hot. The kitchen is squalid, bench stacked with dishes, grains of debris under my bare feet. Flies circle Lulu's bowl, still full from the night before.

'Lulu,' I call out. 'Lulu. Lulu.'

Everything aches. I fumble for coffee and bread. My vision is oddly depthless, a little dark around the edges. I sink into the sofa. The kookaburra alights on his perch outside, pivots his head.

'Lulu,' I call out again. 'Your mate's here, Lulu.'

I can still hear it. It loops in my head while I walk into the kitchen, while I shower, while I make breakfast, while I sit there, listening for the currawongs, calling out again and again to the cat. That loop, those two bars, playing over and over, gently. *Sotto voce.*

While my toast browns and my coffee boils I find myself once again in the upstairs room. Dragging my feet over the carpet, walking in circular motions, spiralling from the centre of the rug to its fringes. Again, my feet find those divots in the pile. Four of them, roughly the leg-span of a grand piano.

I go to my desk. I sip my coffee, swill the hot liquid in my mouth.

My computer is still open where I left it, the same twenty-second loop isolated on the last track. I hit play. Those seven notes. That same cadence, over and over again. I listen: seven notes, descending. Seven notes of a melody.

Take out my little Arturia synth with its single-octave keyboard. Connect it, switch it on. Spread my hand out on the keys.

Seven notes, descending. I feel for them, my fingers reaching into the dark. It starts with an F. EF, those twins, flush to each other, undivided by the black ranks of sharps. FE. FED. FEDC. No. FED A. FED A. FED A. Tentative lower F. FED AF. FED A F. FED A FED. There it is. FED A FED. There it is. FED A FED. FED A FED. Seven notes, tumbling gently downwards, precisely contained by the space of two octaves. My thumb rests next to the low C, the edge of the keys, the edge of my possible knowing.

Seven notes, a short cadence. I play it again in its entirety. I listen. I play. I play. I listen. I know it, but I can't identify it. I play it again and again. Pushing on the door of a locked room.

I let my hand follow it in time. Play and replay, play and replay. Chase it across the keys. With my fingers I extract that melody from where it lives and bring it here.

I play it again and again, and my hand grows colder as the blood drains slowly, as though by retrieving that melody, something of that airless other-space comes with it. I feel it, curling up from the tips of my fingers, quietly surging through my bones as they move in mechanical time.

I play it again and again. My repetition matches tempo with

the playback. They become one sound, one feeling. Then, suddenly, they scatter apart again. It becomes a call and response – that other hand in that other space plays a bar, I play it back.

I sit down on the bed. Press my feet into the floor, anchoring myself. I press my hands against my thighs, will them to steady. I look out the window. The heads of the agapanthus gently sway.

I eat my lunch on the deck, surveilled by the kookaburra, who sits in his usual spot.

I put on a podcast. It's an old episode of a show that I've heard many times before: two American geeks talking about various cultural obscura. This episode is about palimpsests: ancient manuscripts that have been erased and rewritten, traces of the previous text haunting the successive layers of re-inscription. Under the hosts' banter, I can still hear it. Those seven notes, that descending cadence. It's an interoceptive resonance: I hear it with my body. In my spine, in my tissues, in all my sockets and hollows, faint but persistent.

I keep my phone notifications off when I'm working, but I'm done for the day. When I turn them back on, a volley of texts arrive. There are two from friends in Berlin, asking how I am, the news of the break-up having reached them, I guess. There's one from Marta. There's one (my breath halts in my throat) from Elke.

After a long pause, I open it. It's a voice message. A thin blue waveform and a beckoning arrow. The timestamp tells me it's 7:32 minutes long. A live current shoots hot-cold right through me.

I stare at the message dumbly for a long time, my thumb hovering. Something hits me, suddenly and vehemently, in the kidneys. I pivot to find Lulu, squinting in the sunlight. She butts me again with her head, before flopping onto the deck, belly up, her green eyes roaming skywards.

Marta is working a double. She texted to let me know she gets off at three. *Come meet me at work and we can drive to main beach for a swim, left my togs at home though can u pass by the house and pick them up they hanging on the line, ta.*

I make my way down the hill to 86. I push open the door and head into the empty house. As I enter the kitchen, a breeze disturbs the pages of a newspaper left open on the kitchen bench, sends a flurry of cigarette ash across the counter. Marta's cup, the big cracked black one, sits on the laminate.

I find Marta's swimsuit, hanging on the line where she said it would be. I grab it, along with two towels from the hall cupboard.

On my way out, I pass the old piano. Mike's picture, there where it always was. Annie's urn, there where it always was.

It's not as though I make a conscious decision to sit down at the keys. I just find myself there. My right thumb sitting at middle C. The keys on this old thing are real ivory, Annie had said so many times, being as she was of a certain generation, unembarrassed by the slaughter of rare beasts in the service of human luxury. This piano was a luxury in which she held great pride.

Ivory keys are distinguishable from plastic ones by virtue of the fact that the surface of an ivory veneer is rarely a single piece. A hairline fissure runs horizontally down the length of the keyboard, visible in the spaces between the flats and sharps. This can make the veneers more vulnerable to breakage. This keyboard has lost three of its ivories, middle C among them.

My first finger rests in that hollow space, against the bare wood. My second and third find D and E, my fourth and fifth hover – as if setting up for a C major scale. Unsurprising that this would be the form my hand would find, without my volition: every lesson, every practice, for so many years, began in this way.

I find those seven notes again. I replay them in my head, and my hand follows. FED A FED. FED A FED. FED A FED.

The piano is badly out of tune. The notes are distorted almost beyond recognition. I play them again and again. FED A FED. FED A FED. FED A FED. At the end of each bar I find my fingers reaching, a full keyboard in front of them now for the first time in living memory, for the next phrase of this melody which I know, which in my gut I know I know.

In this way, gradually, more and more and more of a lost melody comes back to me. FED A FED. FED A FED. FED A FED. The sound moves into my chest. I let myself hum along. This resonance finds the edge of syllables. Of words. Or the intimation of words – words that have been lost, if in fact I ever knew them. This song has words.

My mother had said to me once, when I was very young: *Love comes too fast for us, and leaves the way it comes.* She said this while looking me firmly in the eye, elbows planted on the kitchen table.

I remember those words, then my backpack. Stuffed with clothes and books and sheet music on the backseat of my mother's car. Still in my pyjamas. The twist of her key in the ignition and the high beams blowing up the misty yard. We drove all the way to Marta's house, where she had that nook made up for me in the hallway, with Jack's old mattress and a stack of crochet blankets. I remember sitting in the dark. Straining to hear the low murmur of the two women talking in the other room. When I woke up, in the savage heat of late morning, my mother's car was gone. It wasn't the first time, and it wasn't the last.

Every week she sent money and every week she phoned. And every week her first question was: 'How are your lessons going? What piece are you learning right now?'

Late afternoon in the demountable music room of the local primary school. Jack and Ngaire were at the beach. I was learning a Schubert song. The piano accompaniment. The first in a famous cycle called *Die Winterreise*. A lover's journey through a landscape. A single set of footprints in the snow. *Die Liebe liebt das Wandern.*

I remember playing the right-hand melody, while my teacher sat next to me, playing the left-hand rhythm. Her hand next to mine. She was gently singing the German words. She had a deep voice, scraping over those guttural consonants. I remember struggling to make it past the fifth bar where there is a trill. A moment of ornamental dissonance, which my small hands tripped over every time. Every time, back to the start. Start over. Start over. Start over.

Something else my mother always said: *It's possible for a living person to become a ghost.* Parts of us break off along the way and become imprints in the places we have occupied, or have occupied us. It's possible for a tragedy or a loss to shatter a spirit, fragments strewn far from where the living flesh stands, walks, breathes, eats, fucks, loves and carries on, reshaped by this fracturing. This could be cataclysmic, or it could be slow. I believe she said this with the authority of a woman who knew what it was to lose herself over and over, who had known that as one of the most consistent conditions of her life. She was a ghost long before she left this world. She knew this about herself.

I don't remember most of Mum's deadshit boyfriends but I do remember Peter, that sinewy bastard she was with before I left home the last time. I guess I was fourteen or so when I woke up to find him in our house. For a short while I think they were something close to happy. I remember the first time he beat the shit out of her. And I remember Marta's words to her, as the two of them sat late at night at Marta's table, drinking cup after cup of Nescafé spiked with dark rum. I was on the sofa, pretending to sleep. The clinking of teaspoons and the call of the koels.

'This won't be the last time,' Marta said. 'Those who do it once will do it again.'

And he did do it again, many times. For years, in fact, after that night. I don't remember much of the fights themselves. I learnt to listen out for a particular tone in his voice, a shift in the sound of his footfall, or the way he closed a door or dragged a knife across a plate. When I heard it, I would know a turn was coming and I would head to my room, close the door. Put my headphones in, crank the music. So, no, I don't remember the fights. What I do remember is the curdling silence that came before and after.

He didn't lay a finger on me, Mum saw to that. She was no angel herself: I got plenty of hidings from her for stupid shit; she was full of her own bile and disappointment with life and had her own ways of unleashing it. But she never would have let him or anyone else lay a hand on me. Her body was always there to take the blow, so mine wouldn't have to.

He flogged me once, and only once, when she was out. I remember the date: 12 September 2001. The day after the Twin Towers fell, and everyone's eyes were glued to the news. A week before the state competition that I was practising for.

Mum was at work. I was on the couch, television on, doing my homework. Peter had this mongrel dog. Poorly trained and always filthy. But Peter loved that animal with a paternal ferocity, a not-uncommon trait in damaged men. The dog tried to muscle its stinking heft onto the couch next to me and I pushed it off, frustrated, a little too hard. It twisted a hind leg as it landed and whimpered.

I remember him flying into the room, and I remember him screaming in my face, and I remember screaming back. I remember walking into the kitchen and him following me, feral with rage. I remember trying to exit down the back stairs and his hand on my wrist, jerking my arm in its socket. I remember falling, the biting edge of a concrete step. I remember the pain coming later, much later, as I sat alone on a train and then a bus and then another bus, as I rounded the headland and caught sight of the ocean as the sun was rising, followed that winding road down through the saltbush thickets, past the ferry wharf, past the bowlo, past the chicken shop, past the bakery.

I remember pushing open the door of 86 Caulfield Road, and the sight of Marta at the kitchen bench, fag in hand, reading the paper. I remember her singing faintly and kneading her pounamu, as we both sat on a hospital bench, the spectral bones of my right hand glowing over a lightbox, the doctor pointing to the fracture in my ulna. I had never seen inside my own body before, and it was beautiful.

I remember driving home, my arm in a cast, and pressing the X-rays against the window of the car. Marta and I talked about anything and everything but what had just happened. I remember looking at my X-rays and telling her my latest nerdy fact: I had recently seen a documentary on the history of sound recording and learnt about *Roentgenizdat*, or bone music, records made by Russian bootleggers using discarded X-ray films, of music that was banned in the Soviet Union.

'Really?' she said. 'On X-rays?' I remember her smiling as we drove. 'Wild.'

My right hand rests on the keys. Still, and suddenly heavy. I turn my listening inwards: to the shallow beat of my breath, to my thumping pulse.

My phone buzzes and I jump. I open it to find another text message from Elke. Another voice message, 9:42 minutes long this time.

The messages will keep coming. They will get longer, and more frantic. It will be Elke, slurring in Denglish into the mic, her mouth too close, her voice too loud. It will be apologies. At first.

I close the messages. I see where Elke's name appears in my inbox. Her name – that name I've said so many times in love and in anger and in exhortation, spoken again and again and again, and brought again and again into flesh, into my flesh, by this intonation, that name which I found so much of myself anchored to, two syllables: *El-Kuh*. That name which, when I speak it now, sinks like a stone.

The whole four years of our togetherness – all of it – is archived under that name. I hold my thumb down on that name. Slide it to the left, until the red trash icon appears.

I sit at the bus stop opposite the ferry wharf and wait for that one bus, that one damn bus that comes through town a handful of times a day, to take me up the hill to the old folks' home, Marta's work.

It's a ten-minute ride up the headland. I get off the bus and start walking up the path towards the big pink building on the hill. Through a set of gates with *Corona Heights* in a scrolling font.

I see Marta from the bottom of the lawn, standing at the building's entrance. Her outline: arms crossed, feet planted wide, smoking and watching the horizon. She gives a little wave when she sees me approach.

'I got your finger buns,' I say.

She assesses the bag in my hand. 'They the plain ones? Or they got the squashed flies?'

'Plain,' I say.

She nods her approval. Stubs out her fag.

We sit for a bit on a bench overlooking the sea. A crowd of gulls have assembled around our feet. Marta stares them down.

She suddenly says, 'Do you remember that game that you and Jack used to play when you were kids?' The edges of her voice flirting with a laugh.

'Which one?'

'The one where one of you would lie under a beach towel and the other one would tip a serve of hot chips over the top and a pack of gulls would come and peck them all off? And the one under the towel would be squirming and screaming.' Marta cackles.

I do remember that game. It was one of Jack's inventions. I remember rolling out from under the towel in hysterics and seeing Jack in his boardies, his bare back on the patchy grass, skinny legs askance. Coiled in a spasm of laughter. Ngaire, ten years old, wet hair, mouth full of something, cracking up and begging to go next.

Marta wishes they were closer to her, her babies. She takes another bite of a finger bun, flicks a few bits of stray coconut from the edge of her navy-blue polo shirt. She takes a good, long look at me, and says nothing.

Some time passes. We smoke and talk.

I say to her: 'Are we gonna get out of here? Isn't your shift over.'

She shrugs. 'No rush for now. It's nice up here this time of day. Sometimes I like to linger in the sun a bit. I don't get to see much of the million-dollar view when I'm inside wiping bums.'

She greets and chats with the residents as they go by, alone, in pairs or in the company of other nurses, on their afternoon walks around the grounds.

As they pass, she gives me the gossip on all of them. She says a sunny hello to Mr Lawson, before adding *racist old cunt* under her breath once he's past. She waves to Mrs Cathcart, who I learn was the headmistress of an Anglican girls' school and a Commonwealth bronze medallist for high diving. Mrs Lee, a diminutive woman with bright eyes and a hot pink tracksuit, had been a publican. She ran four hotels in and around the inner city and two out bush. *Party girl*, Marta tells me.

'This is a bloody palace, this place,' she says. 'Private. Not like some of the other places I've worked in. Jesus. Make your blood run cold.'

I look at Marta's profile. The proud curves of her face. I wonder how her face will change in the coming decades. Her hair has greyed at the temples and her chest has gotten wheezier, but other than that she's barely aged. I remember her and my mother, drunk out of their skulls one night, laughing like kids, teasing me and Jack and Ngaire. *Just you wait till we're toothless in fucken diapers, you little shits. We'll get our own back.* I couldn't imagine Marta as an old woman then. I still can't.

My mother, on the other hand. The last time I saw her she looked ancient beyond her forty-seven years. It wasn't anything special, that meeting. Just a breakfast in a nondescript cafe, near Central station somewhere. I recall she ate an omelette with a side of bacon and we didn't talk much. We never did. I said goodbye to her at the bus stop on George Street. I wonder, if I had known that would have been the last time I'd see her, whether that meeting would have been different at all.

Another nurse approaches, supporting a woman on the crook of her arm. The two of them sit down next to us on the bench.

'Good afternoon, Mrs Egert,' Marta says, louder than usual. She cranes her head over me so she can make full eye contact with the woman, who stares at her blankly.

Mrs Egert doesn't move or speak. She just looks out at the horizon, fine strands of bobbed grey hair shifting around the still contours of her face.

The other nurse chats away to Mrs Egert, who responds with the occasional nod but not much else.

Marta leans in close to my ear and says, 'Mrs Egert is mostly non-verbal. Dementia, rheumatoid arthritis, almost completely deaf. She has moments when the lights go back on.'

I glance at Mrs Egert out of the corner of my eye. I notice her lips are faintly moving, and her eyes are now closed. As though she might be talking or singing to herself.

'There's a complicated woman in there,' Marta goes on. 'I'll tell you the truth: this is not really an adequate facility for advanced dementia patients. Those gates are open all the time, you know. And she's tough, physically, that one. She's busted out of this joint on her own more than once. Couple of times she's gotten as far as the ferry wharf. One of the staff found her down there on her own, walking on the beach by herself. Her and her sister used to walk down the beach every day together, they were quite the pair around town in their time. Her sister was sharp as a tack till the day she dropped dead. I knew her actually, back when I first started nursing – she was a matron at the base hospital. Tough bitch. She was her sister's carer, for the last years she was alive. This one, she was a music teacher. Do you remember her, actually?' She pauses to think for a moment. 'Might have been before your time, I reckon.'

She shakes her head. 'My memory's going.' She pulls a Longbeach from her pack and struggles to light it in the wind.

I turn. I can't see her face. Only the neat box pleats of her skirt, and her hands resting on her knees. I sense her swivel to face me. I feel her cut-glass gaze. I look down. Down at the grass. In my peripheral vision I can see her hands. My hands. Resting in parallel. The deep, burnished glow of that amber ring, proud on the middle finger of her left hand. I notice, finally, the pale crosshatchings across her knuckles and wrists. Her hands. My hands. Resting.

Marta clocks me looking. She puffs and keeps talking, quietly. 'I'll tell you a gnarly story?'

'Sure.'

'She lost her motor skills and her hearing first, and her mind started to go quickly after that. She got real angry and scared, the way people do when that starts. Her sister came up to find her in the music room of their place one day, bleeding all over the piano keys. The pain in her hands was too much so she went for them with a Stanley knife. She's been with us since then.'

'Jesus.'

'Music was most of what she had, I guess.' She stuffs the last, nubby end of a finger bun in her mouth, picks up her cigarettes and her jersey and puts them in her bag. 'Getting old is fucked. You ready to go, kiddo?'

I nod. As I gather up my bag, I'm still aware of Mrs Egert. Her presence beside me. From the corner of my eye, I see her left hand drawing suddenly into a clenched fist.

Marta sets off down the hill. As I get up to follow her, I feel something cold grasp my wrist. I look down and see the woman's hand clasped in mine.

I stare at her directly. Into her bright green eyes. Something – something close to a smile – moves over the surface of her face. I can feel an object, small and hard, pressed between my palm and hers.

The nurse looks at me apologetically and prises the woman's hand from mine. 'Time to say goodbye, Mrs Egert,' she says. 'Let's get you inside.'

I catch up with Marta. We talk and laugh. I'm walking in front of her and I turn around just as she pulls the pin out of her tight bun and her curls erupt in the breeze. She's so beautiful, her face framed by all that wild black.

Without looking at it, I feel the object in my palm. Its weight. With the tip of a finger, I trace the edge of the fine metal band. The smooth face of that resinous stone.